"What Makes [...]
Can [...]

Ben asked.

"Because my life was in your hands from the time you found me," she replied quietly.

His grin faded and he studied her solemnly, his dark-eyed gaze direct and disturbing. She was aware of him as a man, remembering clearly the moment in his kitchen when he had been about to kiss her. And she had wanted him to kiss her.

"Jennifer, I may know something about you," he said quietly, and she felt as if she were about to step into a cavern filled with unknown terrors. A chilling premonition gripped her.

"From your tone, maybe I'm better off not knowing," she said.

And the look he shot her confirmed her suspicions.

Dear Reader:

Welcome to Silhouette Desire®—provocative, compelling, contemporary love stories written by and for today's woman. These are stories to treasure.

Each and every Silhouette Desire is a wonderful romance in which the emotional and the sensual go hand in hand. When you open a Desire™, you enter a whole new world— a world that has, naturally, a perfect hero just waiting to whisk you away! A Silhouette Desire can be light-hearted or serious, but it will always be satisfying.

We hope you enjoy this Desire today—and will go on to enjoy many more.

Please write to us:

Jane Nicholls
Silhouette Books
PO Box 236
Thornton Road
Croydon
Surrey
CR9 3RU

Falcon's Lair

SARA ORWIG

™SILHOUETTE

Desire®

*Silhouette, Silhouette Desire and Colophon
are registered trademarks of Harlequin Books S.A.,
used under licence.*

*First published in Great Britain 1996
Silhouette Books, Eton House, 18-24 Paradise Road,
Richmond, Surrey TW9 1SR*

© Sara Orwig 1995

ISBN 0 373 05938 8

22-9611

*Printed and bound in Great Britain
by Mackays of Chatham PLC, Chatham*

SARA ORWIG

lives with her husband and children in Oklahoma. She has a
patient husband who will take her on research trips any-
where from big cities to old forts. She is an avid collector of
Western history books. With a master's degree in English,
Sara writes historical romance, mainstream fiction and contemporary romance. Books are beloved treasures that take
Sara to magical worlds, and she loves both reading and
writing them.

To Lucia Macro with many thanks.

One

"Where do mountain lions go when it snows?"

Ben Falcon looked down at the five-year-old boy buckled into the seat beside him. Wipers on the Jeep clacked rhythmically as snow tumbled from the gray skies.

"Renzi, I don't know where they go. Maybe they have caves they get into. They have thick fur coats though, so they don't get cold."

"I want to see a mountain lion. I haven't ever seen one."

"We have them around here. You'll see one sometime."

"I won't if I have to go back to the city."

Ben glanced at him, knowing he seldom mentioned his mother or going back to live with her. He felt a pang of sadness and reached over to give Renzi's shoulder a squeeze. The boy's big brown eyes gazed up at him with such trust and love that Ben felt another ache for the child. How could his mother not care about him or want him?

Ben followed the curve in the road and saw the low-lying buildings spread across the valley, their roofs white with snow, smoke curling from chimneys. The Bar-B Ranch for boys who needed temporary homes away from homes. From the first afternoon he had met Lorenzo Lopez, Ben had been drawn to the child and now occasionally took Renzi to stay overnight for several days at his ranch, which bordered along the south boundary of the boys' ranch.

Ben halted the Jeep as the tall director strode outside. Blond, cheerful and energetic, Derek Hansen pulled his parka closer around his face and waved.

Ben returned the wave and looked at Renzi who had unbuckled his belt and was fastening his parka. He gazed up at Ben and threw his arms around him. "Thank you, Ben, for letting me stay with you."

Ben hugged the small boy in return. "We'll do it again soon, Renzi. I'll see you Sunday."

"Thanks." Renzi slid across the seat as Ben reached over him and opened the door. Renzi climbed out, waving at Derek as he ran past him into the building.

Ben lowered a window. "He seemed to have a good time."

"I know he had a good time," Derek said. "Thanks for giving him the extra attention."

"I wish I could more of them. It's the first week of April, and from reports I'm getting, we're in for another hell of a blizzard."

"I don't think Mother Nature knows it's supposed to be spring. You take care going home." Derek stepped back and Ben swung the Jeep around and drove away. He passed two boys riding horseback and he waved, seeing them wave in return. The world became a white blur, snow bending the limbs of the dark spruce that lined the county road as he headed back to his place.

Finally Ben turned his Jeep along the last grinding climb up the mountainside toward his ranch house perched in the Sangre de Cristo range of the Rockies. Snowflakes swirled on the sigh of the wind while the Jeep's motor roared in the silence. The road curved, the land dropped away to the east and Ben's gaze swept the white world, the dark treetops below him. His eyes narrowed as a flash of orange caught his attention.

"What the devil?"

A lick of fire danced skyward, flames shooting up and black smoke spreading. Stunned, Ben stared in amazement, and then he jammed his foot on the brake, calculated where the fire was and swore under his breath as he threw the Jeep into reverse.

Some damned tourist was on his property and had gone off the mountain! The car must be burning.

He made the tight turn, the Jeep's wheels inches from the edge that dropped away for hundreds of feet down the mountain. Then he jammed his foot on the gas pedal, skidding down the twisting road, snow flying out behind the wheels as the Jeep took the snaking curves.

Winding his way as swiftly as possible, he descended to the valley. Knowing every inch of his land, he turned off onto what he knew was a narrow dirt lane beneath the snow.

Seldom had he wanted a cellular phone on hand, but now he wished he had one so he could call 911 and let the highway patrol handle this one.

He slowed, easing his way over rough terrain, following splashing Flint Creek, tall spruce and bare-limbed aspen blocking his view of the blaze. Moments later he spotted the fire through the trees and drew a deep breath. The highway patrol couldn't save anyone caught in the conflagration, and the flames looked as if they would hit the gas tank at any moment.

Ben climbed out of the Jeep to approach the car, his skin prickling because he expected an explosion. On the ground near the car something dark shifted. He frowned, drawing a swift breath as he looked at a mass of thick hair like a slash of chestnut against the white snow. A woman was sprawled facedown only a few feet from the fire, the orange flames bathing over her.

While he raced toward the prone figure, panic swept him because the car was going to blow any moment now. Suddenly she pushed up and struggled to her feet. With a cry she pitched forward. Stretching out his long legs, he caught her.

"Easy. I've got you."

"Got to go—" she gasped, struggling to get free of him. With another sharp cry, she sagged against him, and he swung her up in his arms, feeling a rush of admiration because she wasn't crying hysterically, but was fighting to keep going.

"We have to get away from the car," he said.

"Help," she whispered, snow beading her dark lashes, falling on her pink cheeks as she looked into his eyes. A cut left a thin scarlet line across her cheek to her jaw. Her arms went around his neck, clinging tightly.

Ben whirled around, running with her, and she placed her head against his chest. A protective urge that he hadn't felt in years made him clasp her tightly against his body. She was soft and smelled of springtime. Locks of her silky hair blew across his jaw and he felt a pang, realizing it had been a long time since he had carried a woman in his arms. Desperate, he stretched out his legs, trying to get as much distance as possible between them and the car.

A loud blast behind him threw him forward. He went down, trying to cover her body with his own. For an instant he was aware of the supple curves beneath him, long legs tangling with his, her softness. He looked down at her as she stared at him, her green eyes seeming to pull him into their endless cool depths.

Something hit his shoulder with a blow that felt as if a hammer had pounded into him. He felt a sharp pain and glanced back at a burning hunk of material lying on his leg. He kicked it away, rolling in the snow to extinguish his burning jeans.

When Ben turned to the woman, she lay sprawled on her back in the snow, her lashes dark shadows above her cheeks, her face pale, a crimson stain showing where her dark green slacks were ripped. Cuts were across her hands, on her cheeks, and a sleeve of her navy parka was ripped, hanging loosely and revealing her scraped and bleeding arm. Ignoring the pain that shot across his shoulder, he picked her up again. Turning his back on the wreck, he rushed toward his Jeep.

Gently he placed the woman in the back of the Jeep and threw a blanket over her. "You shouldn't have been driving in this storm. You don't belong here anyway," he grumbled, frowning because of her stillness. He wondered why she was here. The nearest resort was at Rimrock, forty miles to the west, and the small town of Concho to the southeast seldom drew anyone along the rugged stretch of state highway near his place. And she had been on private property, driving on the road to his house. He guessed she had gotten lost. Either that or car trouble had caused her to look for help. He slid his hand beneath her coat and felt her pulse. To his relief, it was steady.

"Snow blinded you?" he asked, brushing a lock of red hair away from her forehead. A tiny smattering of freckles covered her nose, giving her a young, vulnerable look. He yanked out his handkerchief and dabbed at the blood on her cheek. "Crazy lady," he said softly. "You shouldn't have been driving in the storm. I'll take you home where it's warm, and let's hope you don't have internal injuries or broken bones that need a doc. If you do, we'll have to call for the emergency chopper. In the meantime," he said, placing his knuckles against her throat in an uncustomary tender gesture, "you're going where no woman has gone before," he said quietly, thinking about his mountain home and the privacy he guarded so fiercely.

He climbed out and went around the Jeep to slide beneath the wheel. "I need to get you where it's warm," he said, wondering about this sudden urge he felt to talk to her even though she was unconscious. Maybe it was the woman's silence that compelled him to talk. Or a feeling that by talking to her, she wouldn't sink deeper into unconsciousness.

Usually he resented any intrusion into his privacy and sent trespassers scurrying away with a scathing remark or look. Even beautiful trespassers. When he wanted a woman, he would find one on his own terms.

He put the Jeep in gear and wound his way back to the road. By the time he was climbing the last quarter mile to his home, daylight was gone. Large flakes of snow spiraled against the windshield, spinning in the twin beams of headlights.

When he finally slowed in front of his house, a husky bounded forward, barking as Ben braked and climbed out. "Down, Fella. We've got a guest, and she's hurt."

Ben leaned into the back and as gently as possible, lifted the woman into his arms, cradling her against his chest. Locks of her red hair curled against his sheepskin-lined coat. Large flakes fell and caught on her lashes and dotted her hair. Ben tightened his arms, holding her close. She was limp and unconscious and he worried about her, glancing at the gash in her thigh. With care he carried her in long-legged strides toward the dark bulk of his log house that looked as rustic and natural as the trees surrounding it.

As soon as he opened the door, the dog bounded past him into a wide, comfortable room decorated in deep reds and blues with a polished plank floor and braided rugs scattered across the room and in front of the fireplace.

Kicking the door closed, Ben carried the woman through the front room to the large bedroom that ran along the back of the house, its floor-to-ceiling glass giving a panoramic view of the snow-swept mountains and the wide valley. Without giving the windows a glance, he crossed to the king-size bed and knelt to ease her down as the husky curled up in front of the fireplace.

Yanking back the covers, Ben held the woman against him as he sat her up to pull off her bulky navy parka. A green sweater clung to curves that made him pause while his gaze wandered down over her enticing fullness. He lowered her to the bed and removed her fur-lined boots.

Easing away a boot, he frowned as he looked at her swollen ankle. Each brush against her bare skin was evidence of her chill from the cold and shock. In a lithe movement, he crossed the room and piled logs in the large stone fireplace. In minutes a fire blazed as he returned to her. He stared down at her, knowing he had to peel away her slacks and bandage her wounded thigh. With sure fingers he unbuttoned the soft woolen slacks and slid down the zipper.

"Sorry, lady, but you need help, and this is the only way you're going to get that wound bandaged." He eased down the slacks and the ripped panty hose, unable to keep his gaze from drifting over creamy skin, her flat stomach and a clinging, pink lace teddy that did little to hide the thick auburn curls at the juncture of her thighs.

He felt his body responding with an intensity that shocked him. His gaze shifted to the gash across her right thigh. Ben went to the adjoining bathroom to get what he needed for first aid.

Seated beside her, with a warm, damp cloth to wipe away the blood, he paused when his hands touched her smooth, cool skin. She was too cold—probably chilled to the bone and in shock—and he knew he should work quickly and get her covered. As he tended her, he tried to ignore the steady throb of his shoulder because her injuries required his attention first.

Her arm was scraped, and as he pushed the sweater high he felt for broken bones. While he probed carefully, he was aware of the delicacy of her bones, the blue vein throbbing in her slender neck. He placed his hand against her throat and was reassured by her steady pulse.

Too aware of her long-limbed beauty, he bandaged her thigh and shifted on the bed to lift her leg and clean a scrape along her shapely calf. As smooth as silk, her flesh was warming beneath his hands, and he was intensely aware of every bare inch exposed to him. His body responded in a manner that was intense, and he paused, flicking a glance over her again, over the flimsy bit of pink, up to her face.

"You're lucky to be alive," he said quietly to her as he worked. Her eyes were closed, her full lips rosy in spite of the paleness of her skin. Dark bruises were beginning to show on her face and legs and arms.

As the fire crackled and roared, the room grew hot and perspiration beaded Ben's brow. He yanked away his jacket and sweater, baring his muscled chest. He sat close against her hip, holding her hand to pick away fragments of glass and clean tiny cuts, aware how slender and delicate her pale fingers looked against his callused, tanned ones. He placed an ice pack against her swollen ankle and elevated her foot on a pillow.

With care he pushed her sweater high to feel for broken ribs, pressing gently, sliding the tips of his fingers over her satiny flesh, too aware of the rise of her breasts only inches away, his hand brushing the soft fullness and sending currents of prickly awareness through him. Satisfied nothing was broken, he slipped the sweater down again.

When he finished ministering to her, he pulled up the covers, his gaze traveling up her long legs, pausing a moment on the thick triangle of curls, then drifting higher over the sweater. As he studied her, his body heated until he felt as if he were standing in flames.

He glanced back at the roaring fire. The husky raised his head and looked at his master. "The lady's very pretty, Fella," Ben said to the dog, which thumped its tail.

She moaned softly, and Ben stroked her hair away from her face, sitting down beside her. "You're all right," he said quietly. "Damned lucky to be alive. If I hadn't found you—" He paused, his brow furrowing when he remembered the explosion. Even if she had survived the blast, if she had spent the night on the mountain, she might have died from exposure.

"You're safe and warm and you're going to be fine. And when the storm ends and you're well, I'll take you to Rimrock where you were probably headed." As he talked to her, he traced his finger down along her jaw, avoiding touching bruises. Now she was warming, the heat of her body beginning to feel normal to his touch. He felt a surge of relief and then told himself he was being idiotic. She was a total stranger who was probably on her way to meet her lover. Ben reminded himself that she didn't mean anything to him.

He already knew there was no wedding ring on her finger. Annoyed with himself, he shifted his weight. He was having an acute uncustomary reaction to this stranger.

"Maybe I feel like I saved you, so now I should protect you," he said softly, inhaling the sweet lilac scent that lingered about her.

Ben stood and crossed to the bathroom to look at himself in a full-length mirror. His shoulder was dark with a bruise, a lump swelling across his back. He had a cut on his temple, which he hadn't felt. He pushed back his thick black hair, and examined the dark skin of his face—a heritage from the long-ago Comanche blood. He stripped away the T-shirt, unbuckled his belt and peeled his jeans from narrow hips, muscles rippling as he pulled off mud-spattered boots. Tossing aside his briefs, he stepped beneath a hot shower and winced when the water hit his injured shoulder.

In minutes when he was dry, dressed in a clean pair of jeans and socks, he walked back to the bed to look down at her.

She stirred, moaned and her eyes flew open. Caught in their green depths, Ben felt an electric jolt as he gazed at her. Her straight reddish brown brows drew together and she sat up, gasping with pain. Her eyes widened and a look of terror filled them.

"I have to go—" she gasped, pushing away covers. "I have to find him."

Barely hearing her words, Ben sat down beside her and leaned gently against her shoulders, catching her fluttering hands in his. "Shh. You've been in a car wreck, and we're in the storm of the year. You're safe here."

"No! I have to go now!" Her agitation increased.

"You're not going out in this storm. And you can't stand, either. Your ankle is hurt," he said forcefully. Holding her, feeling her warm, delicate shoulders beneath his hands, Ben wondered when she would discover she was only half-dressed.

"No! I have to—" she cried, pushing against him, trying to sit up and crying out. She grabbed her side. "Oh!"

"You're hurt," he said, his broad chest blocking her. He didn't want to frighten her or make her think his intentions were bad. For a moment he had to laugh at himself. Since when had he become so damned trustworthy with a beautiful woman? His cynical thought disappeared as he tried to struggle with her without hurting her.

She pushed against him and twisted away suddenly, lunging across the bed. He reached to catch her, scrambling over the bed as she swung her feet down.

"My clothes!" she gasped, giving him an angry look when she stepped off the bed. When she put her weight on her foot, a cry tore from her and she would have fallen, but he caught her, his arm going behind her shoulders, the other arm beneath her warm thighs. He swung her up against his bare chest, leaning forward to place her on the bed again.

She struggled against him. "Be still," he ordered, and green eyes stared at him defiantly, yet she became quiet.

"I took your slacks off because your leg is cut and bleeding. You can't walk—"

"Have to go," she murmured as he covered her and sat beside her, pushing hair away from her face. Sitting up, she waved her hands in a futile protest, determination in her eyes as she stared at him. "Have to find Ben Falcon now—"

Stunned, Ben felt a jolt. He shifted away from her as quickly as if he had discovered a rattler in his bed. His breath went out in a hiss and he stood, his brows becoming thunderclouds while his scowl deepened and all his protectiveness toward her changed to a churning rage.

Two

Ben stared at the woman as she looked around in uncertainty, and then her eyes closed and she lay back on the bed again.

Frowning, he placed his hands on his hips. "Dammit," he said quietly, thinking how he had brought her here. He should have guessed, yet it had been almost four years since Weston had come after him or sent someone after him. Long enough that Ben thought his father had given up trying to get him home.

Ben wanted Weston's woman out of his house and his life. For a few minutes, an image of Andrea danced in mind, and the terrible anger he had felt when he had discovered she had been picked by Weston as the perfect match. The first few years after buying the ranch, he'd had damn little time to have even a casual date, and after the stormy relationship of his parents, Ben had no inclination to rush into any lasting commitment, but the last couple of years he found the long, lonely winter nights making him think about going to town and seeking companionship. His gaze slid back to the woman.

Angered, he turned and walked to the window as he tried to gain control of his emotions. Snow swirled and fell against the glass, some sticking in frosty white blotches. Ben's thoughts drifted back to his childhood, to the abusive father he had clashed with as far back as he could remember.

Weston set impossible demands and Ben was the oldest of two sons, never able to satisfy his father's demands. Ben rebelled before he was ten years old and from that time on it was war between them, with Weston bullying, threatening, punishing, doing everything in his power to break Ben's stubborn determination to live his own life. And he thought about Geoff, his younger brother, who had tried to please their father and live up to impossible demands until he'd been killed trying to win a speedboat race sponsored by Falcon Enterprises.

The last time Weston had come after him, Ben had spent six months in a Texas jail for assaulting the hired men sent to force him to go home. Within two hours after arrest, his father had appeared and offered to get him out immediately if he would go to work in the family company. But Ben had refused, preferring jail to life under his father's impossible demands. He thought of all the people Weston had sent to bring him back—detectives, cops, strong-arm toughs, beautiful women.

Ben's thoughts shifted and he turned to look at the woman. How much was she going to pay? Would her body be part of the bargain? Maybe it was because of her momentary vulnerability, but she didn't look like the flashy, high-dollar call girls Weston had sent to lure him back when Ben had been in his twenties.

Now as he calmed, Ben's brows drew together. She had looked right at him and said she had to get to Ben Falcon.

He frowned and moved back to the bed. She was determined to get to him, yet she hadn't recognized him. His father would have coached her, briefed her and given her pictures.

"Dammit," Ben said and leaned over her, sliding his hand over her head. He felt the lump on her head beneath her hair and realized he'd been so busy looking for broken bones and tending her cuts, he hadn't felt for bumps on her head easily hidden by her riotous red hair. He glanced at the snow again and crossed the room to the phone to punch 911.

In minutes he had made arrangements for the medical chopper from Albuquerque to fly to his ranch and pick up the woman and get her to Emergency. Next he called his physician friend, Kyle Whittaker, to ask him if he would meet them at the hospital.

Dressed in a black sweater and jeans, Ben gathered up his keys, pushed his wallet into his hip pocket while he punched a number and told Zeb Diez, his foreman, what had happened and where he was going. "I'll light up the grounds where the chopper lands. You turn the lights off when we're gone."

"Sure, boss." Zeb's deep voice sounded alert. "We're going to have to get feed to the animals in this storm."

"You know where the keys are to the Jeep if you need it. And check with Derek to see if they need any supplies," Ben said, staring at the gray night sky and thinking about the boys' ranch. In weather like this they wouldn't be able to get supplies in and would rely on Ben or his men.

"I'll check on them," Zeb answered.

"I'll call you as soon as I know when I'll be back," Ben promised, replacing the receiver and glancing at his watch. He had agreed to be ready and waiting for the chopper.

He picked up her jacket, searching the pockets, looking at the label. Next he picked up the slacks and repeated the process, pulling out a torn, folded slip of paper. It was a page from a memo pad with the name Jennifer printed in blue at the top. He stuffed the paper into his own pocket and walked over to the bed.

"C'mon, Jennifer or whoever you are—we're going for a ride," he said in a tight, angry voice. Yet he worked slowly and with care as he eased her slacks back on her, lifting her slim thighs as he slid the dark wool up over them, trying to avoid letting his gaze roam to the pink lace. He slid his hands beneath her soft, round bottom, his breath catching while his manhood swelled and hardened. He tugged the slacks up to her waist, buttoning them and feeling his body respond as intensely as if he had been undressing her. When he pushed back the covers, she groaned and opened her eyes, staring at him and frowning. She rubbed her head.

"Where am I?"

"I'm Ben Falcon," he said carefully, watching her closely.

She frowned and rubbed her head. "Ben," she said hesitantly, "I know you, don't I?"

"I saw your car go off the road and found you and brought you here." Her green eyes had a crystal clearness that at the moment held a troubled vulnerability. "I'm Ben," he continued, "and you're—?"

She rubbed her forehead again. "I'm—" She paused and looked up at him and shook her head. "I don't know," she said in a whisper. "I can't think. My head hurts...."

"I found a slip of paper in your pocket that had the name Jennifer written on it, so I guess we'll go with that."

"Jennifer," she said quietly, while shaking her head and frowning. "I don't know."

"You have a bump on your head. I've called an Albuquerque hospital. They're flying a chopper here, and I told them we'd be ready and waiting. Relax and don't worry. You'll be in good hands. I have an orthopedic friend who'll meet us in Emergency."

"I don't remember. I remember snow. So much snow. My friend Mary." She paused and looked up. "Mary is my friend."

"Mary who?"

She thought and shook her head. "Do you have my purse?"

He sat down on the bed, still feeling the deep-running current of anger, yet right now she looked frightened and in need of comfort and a friend. He took her hand in his. "You were traveling in a snowstorm and went off the mountain, wrecking your car. The car burned, and I didn't see a purse when I found you. I'll go back tomorrow and look to see what I can find."

"I'm lots of trouble for you."

"No, you're not," he said, rubbing his thumb across her knuckles. She looked down at his dark-skinned fingers holding her slender, pale ones.

"I don't remember anything," she said softly, frowning at him while worry clouded her eyes. "Thank you for helping me."

"You'll be all right," he said gruffly. "Here's your coat. Probably when shock from the wreck wears off, you'll remember everything."

She brightened and touched his cheek. Her fingers were cool and light on his skin. Startled, he felt an uncustomary awareness from such a slight, casual touch. "You're hurt," she said quietly. "Is that from trying to help me?" she asked, running her finger alongside the cut on his temple.

"It's only a scratch."

"You must have been in danger to get bruised and scratched like that. Thank you for taking me in and caring for me. You're patient and kind," she remarked, and smiled at him, revealing even white teeth and a dimple in her left cheek.

Startled, Ben was aware that never before had a woman told him that he was patient or kind. There was a trusting look in her eyes that tore at him because he couldn't forget why she was in his bedroom. When her memory returned, she would not call him kind and he wouldn't tolerate her in his house.

"I'll put on my coat," he said, standing and walking away from her, feeling as if he had moved away from warmth and sunshine, yet at the same time annoyed by the sensation. He yanked on his sheepskin parka, stuffed leather gloves in his pocket and jammed a broad-brimmed black Stetson on his head. Picking up her parka, he turned to find her watching him.

He crossed to the bed and she sat up, swinging her feet over the side. She paused, studying her slacks. "Did I dream I tried to get out of bed?"

"No. I caught you when you fell, and helped you back to bed. You've injured your ankle."

"I didn't think I was dressed," she said, her cheeks flushing slightly.

"I took off your slacks to tend to your injured thigh, but when I saw we had to go to the hospital in Albuquerque, I put your slacks back on you," he said in what he hoped was an impersonal tone. Her blush deepened while she looked away.

As he helped her into the coat, his fingers brushed her nape and her shoulders and he was intensely aware of each contact. She slanted him a thoughtful glance.

"I feel as if I've known you a long time."

"I never met you before your car wrecked on my property," he said evenly, trying to keep his voice impassive and curb his anger.

She frowned and bit her lip, and his gaze was drawn to the small, even white teeth that bit slightly into her rosy, full underlip. As he watched her, the pink tip of her tongue touched her upper lip and he felt desire stir, a curiosity to lean down and taste her lips and tongue and mouth that looked so enticing.

"I don't have any difficulty remembering your name."

He shrugged and began to fasten the front of her coat, zipping it closed as if she were a child. "I remember how to do that," she said with a trace of amusement, and he looked into her eyes, seeing a warmth that made him like her in spite of her errand.

He smoothed her collar, brushing her hair back from her face, suddenly reluctant to move away from her. The moment he realized what he was doing, he stood, pushing up his sleeve to look at his watch.

"Let's go to the kitchen to wait." When he picked her up, she slid her arm around his neck. He tried to ignore the pleasant fit of her in his arms as well as her delicate scent that was growing familiar now.

"Where am I?"

"You're in northern New Mexico in the mountains."

"That means nothing to me," she said with panic in her voice. "I don't remember where I live or my name or why I'm here. Would you know if I lived near you?"

"You don't. I own a spread of land on this mountain and along the valley—I raise cattle. The only other people in the valley are boys on a ranch for homeless kids."

"I don't know why I was driving in this storm, but I feel as if there's something I need to do."

He crossed through the kitchen and hooked his toe beneath a bar stool to pull it out and set her on it. "We'll wait here for the chopper. I expect it within the next five minutes." The husky followed them into the room, walking up to the woman and wagging his tail. As she scratched his ears, his tail wagged faster.

"His name's Fella." Ben handed her gloves to her and flipped the parka over her head, fastening it beneath her chin. She watched him solemnly, and he felt caught in the probing look, feeling an electric tension spark between them. His fingers stilled while her gaze seemed to wrap around him and pull him closer into a warmth that he needed.

His gaze lowered to her mouth, and then he raised his eyes back to hers. Fire danced in the emerald depths, and her eyelids drooped in a sensual look. His heart pounded in his chest, and he felt as if danger threatened him while at the same time, desire was as hot as a flame curling inside him. He slid his hand beneath her hood behind her neck, pulling her head toward him as his gaze lowered to her mouth again.

"We're strangers," she whispered.

"That might make it better," he answered in a husky, cynical voice.

"I know I can trust you with my life," she said solemnly, "because I wouldn't have survived out there in the storm."

He was torn between wanting to savage her mouth, to take her lips and kiss her with all the passion and anger and curiosity he felt, to let her know she had voluntarily sought out the wolf in his lair and she would have to pay the price. At the same time, her eyes were trusting and warm with a sensuality that should be savored—a combination of innocent trust and womanly certainty that rocked him and made him want to brush her lips lightly with his own. He wanted to take care and time to ignite the passion that he suspected she was capable of. The thought startled him, and he wondered why he felt that way about her when he didn't even know her.

His gaze was locked with hers again and he saw her reaction; she wanted his kiss. *Was* she one of the high-priced call girls, the thousand-dollar-a-night babes his father thought would entice him? Or one of the special ones who played for higher stakes, trying to win his heart because of Weston's money? Anger surged and then ebbed as he looked down at her lips and slowly leaned his head closer. Her lashes lowered, and she closed her eyes while she placed her palms against his chest.

The pulsating clatter of the helicopter's motor grew louder, cutting into the spell and making Ben swear silently as he paused only inches from her. She turned her head toward the door.

"Here comes the helicopter." The note of fear in her voice was mirrored in her eyes when she gripped his hand. "Will you stay with me? You're the only person I know."

"I'll be with you," he promised gruffly, suspecting when memory returned, she would regret keeping him close and guessing that the fear was uncustomary for her. She had been brave—or foolhardy—enough to try to get to his place in a blinding storm, determined enough to feel she could successfully follow Weston's wishes and bring the wayward son home.

Ben picked her up and she wound her arms around his neck again. When he opened the door, the husky bounded outside, barking at the noisy chopper as it set down only yards from the house, a dark bulk in the bright lights and brilliant snow.

Ben hurried to it, climbing inside while medics took her from his arms. Catching a glimpse of Zeb as he strode toward the house, Ben waved and saw Zeb wave in return.

When the chopper lifted, Ben rode beside her, holding her hand in his, aware she kept her gaze on him steadily while they whisked skyward. He glanced down at his place, the snow sparkling in the brightness of the yard lights and then they swept across the darkened land and he saw the shadows of spruce and pine and boulders that were dark against the snow. For an instant he felt a surge of satisfaction that came occasionally when he looked at his land. He had bought the first acres with savings and he was gradually enlarging, determined to carve a life for himself here, far removed from his past.

Like a noisy spinning top, the chopper raced across the night sky to set down outside a hospital in Albuquerque.

When she was taken to Emergency, Ben stood at the admitting desk, filling out papers, signing that he would be responsible for the bills.

"Ben," a deep voice said, and Ben glanced around to see a lanky, white-coated doctor. Ben moved away from the desk to talk to his friend, tall, sandy-haired Kyle Whittaker, who folded his arms and leaned against the wall to listen as Ben related how he had found Jennifer and taken her home.

"She doesn't remember anything, and I didn't find any identification," Ben said, knowing he was holding back on his friend, but he wanted to talk to Weston before the hospital was involved.

"We'll check her over. The memory loss may be gone within hours."

"That's what I figured."

"Since you don't know her, do you want to wait or turn it over to us and the Albuquerque police to locate her family?"

"I'll wait."

Kyle arched a sandy eyebrow and studied Ben. "That's not the answer I expected."

Ben shrugged. "She seems vulnerable right now."

"I'll keep you informed."

Ben nodded and watched him walk away. In minutes Ben finished admittance formalities at the desk and he crossed the lobby to a narrow alcove with pay phones. With one quick call he could get her identity and have someone come pick her up and take her to Dallas where she belonged. He stared at the phone and felt a momentary reluctance as he remembered gazing into her green eyes and recalled the soft touch of her fingers on his cheek.

"Dammit." He swore and picked up the phone, punching numbers. The receiver lifted on the third ring.

"You've reached 555-3210," came an unfamiliar brisk male voice. "We are unable to come to the phone now. Please leave your message, your name, your number, and we will get back with you when possible."

Ben swore again as he waited. A loud beep rang in his ear and he gripped the phone tightly. "Weston, I have to talk to you. You know the number. Your messenger was in a car wreck." Ben slammed down the phone and thought of the executives who worked for his father. He could call one of them, but they wouldn't do anything until his father gave orders.

Then he thought of Mark Kisiel, vice president of Falcon Drilling and a man Ben had always respected. He called Information, got Mark's number and dialed, getting another recorded message. At the sound of the beep, Ben moved closer to the phone. "Mark, this is Ben. The woman messenger has been in a wreck. She isn't badly injured, but she doesn't belong here. Get my father to call. He knows the number." Ben replaced the receiver and stared at the phone, finally deciding he couldn't do anything else until he heard from his father or Mark.

Ben strode toward the double glass doors and stared at the yellow lights in the parking lot. The snow was still falling in the golden circles cast by the lamps, spreading in shiny, wet puddles on the slushy, salt-covered asphalt. He could tell them to contact his father about Jennifer and walk out now, leaving her in the care of the hospital and the police. Instead, he turned around and sat on a vinyl chair, staring at the snow while he waited, suspecting his father's birthday last month had triggered this intrusion. Perhaps Weston was finally facing his own mortality and wanted to try again to bring his son back into the business. Bitterness and a coldness more chilling than the snow filled Ben. He closed his eyes and sat quietly waiting.

"Ben?"

Ben rose and crossed the room to Kyle who was marking something on a chart. "Dr. Hobson checked her, too," Kyle said. "She has a mild concussion, no internal bleeding, no hemorrhaging. She's bruised a rib, sprained her ankle. Beyond that, it's minor cuts and bruises, and you did a nice job of tending her wounds. I want to keep her overnight for observation. In this storm, you can't get out anyway.''

"I can go home in daylight the same way I got in. Put her in a room, and tomorrow I'll charter a chopper to take us home.''

"That'll be a big bill for a total stranger,'' Kyle said, studying him more closely. Ben had known Kyle in college and when Ben had moved to the area, he had been surprised the first time he had broken a rib riding in a rodeo and had encountered Kyle at the hospital. Since then, when Ben was in Albuquerque, they occasionally had lunch together. Ben could count close friends on the fingers of one hand, but the orthopedic surgeon was one of them.

Ben shrugged. "I have to get back to the ranch tomorrow. My cattle will need hay dropped, so I can use the chopper before I send it back. When will her memory return?''

"I didn't tell her—if it doesn't return within two weeks, it may not return at all.'' Kyle tucked the clipboard under his arm. "Where will you stay tonight?''

"I'll get one of those lounge chairs in her room and I'll stay with her.''

Curiosity burned in Kyle's brown eyes, but he merely nodded.

"Kyle, I think my father sent her here,'' Ben said quietly.

Kyle's sandy brows raised in question. "I thought he'd quit coming after you. You know who she is?'' he asked, annoyance creeping into his voice.

"No, I don't, but she drifted in and out of consciousness when I first picked her up, and one time she tried to push me out of the way. She said she had to find Ben Falcon. That's when I realized she didn't remember everything because she didn't recognize me. The next time she regained consciousness, she didn't remember that much.''

"Damn. If she knew your name, he must have sent her. Call him and get him to pick her up.'' Kyle slanted his head, curiosity back in his eyes. "Unless you want to keep her around for a while."

"I did call him while you were checking her over. I couldn't get through—his answering machine took my message—so I called one of his men and left a message. Tomorrow I should get a response."

Kyle shook his head. "Sorry if you're going another nine rounds with him. I'd think by now he would realize you have your own life."

"My father can see things only one way," Ben answered flatly. "Until I hear from him or her memory returns, I'll stay with her."

He received another curious look from Kyle. "You've had sprains before, so you know what to do—ice tonight and tomorrow. Then have her soak her foot in hot water a couple of times a day. Four or five days and her foot should be okay. Still have crutches?"

"Yeah. Will it be worse for her to tell her what I suspect?"

"No, it won't. Go ahead. We'll check on her through the night. If nothing changes, we'll release her early in the morning."

"Okay. Thanks, Kyle, for coming out here in this storm."

"Glad to do it. You'll get a bill," he added with a grin. "She's in room 520 if you want to go see her."

When he entered the silent room that had a small light burning in the adjoining bathroom, he closed the door quietly behind him and moved to the bed.

"Ben?" she asked, turning toward him.

His heart seemed to lurch and stop and then start beating again. She was propped against the pillows, the head of the bed cranked up so she was almost upright. Her flame-colored hair spilled over the pillow and her shoulders. In the white hospital gown she looked more defenseless than before. Her foot was elevated, a lump beneath the sheet.

Jennifer turned, her pulse jumping as Ben Falcon's broad shoulders were a dark silhouette in the wide doorway. This stranger was a lifeline to her. The doctors had been reassuring, and she knew she was fortunate to be alive, from what Ben had said about the wreck, but when she tried to think about the past and nothing came to mind, a cold terror gripped her. She watched the tall man who was little more than a stranger, yet now so important to her. He crossed the room, and she couldn't resist the urge to reach out for his hand.

His strong warm grip was reassuring as his fingers curled around hers, and she covered his hand with her free hand while he leaned one hip against the bed. "Thank you for staying," she said, running her fingers over his large knuckles and reluctantly releasing his hand.

"I'm here and I'll stay with you," he said casually, tossing his coat on the back of the chair and pulling the chair close beside the bed.

"I know I'm interfering in your life."

"It's the middle of the night in a snowstorm, so there's not a lot I could be doing if I were home," he said lightly as he sat down beside her. He touched her hair.

"I feel like there's something I'm supposed to be doing, but I can't recall what it is. Something urgent."

"It'll come to you."

"Ben, I know your name, but I don't know mine."

"You will. From what Kyle told me, you should wake up in the morning and have your memory back."

"They said that I should sit up, and a nurse checks my blood pressure every thirty minutes."

"I'll sit here and talk to you."

Relief surged in her. She knew she was interfering in his life, yet she was thankful to have him with her because she gained a sense of security from his calmness. Deep down she felt as if she had known him before the last few hours even though he had been firm in his answer that they had never met until he found her at the wreck.

"Every time I close my eyes, I feel as if I'll lose you and I'll be all alone in the world."

"I'm here to stay," he said, leaning forward with his elbows propped on his knees. She placed her hand on his shoulder lightly.

"Thank you, Ben. I try not to think about tomorrow. I don't have any money or any family or friends until my memory returns. I don't know how I'll pay for this hospital room."

"I already have."

She raised her head off the pillow abruptly to stare at him. "I'll pay you back. I don't know what job I had, but I must have done something. I remember keeping books and filing taxes—why can I recall my work and not know my name?"

"It'll all come to you," he said with narrowed eyes, as if something she said was causing him thought. "I'll take care of you until you remember."

"You've been good to me, and I know I can trust you. You must be an incredibly good person to take care of a stranger this way."

He startled her with a sudden grin.

"What's funny?"

"What makes you so certain you can trust me?" he asked dryly.

"Because my life was in your hands from the time you found me at the scene of the wreck until the helicopter arrived," she replied quietly.

His grin faded and he studied her solemnly, his dark-eyed gaze direct and disturbing. She was aware of him as a man, remembering clearly the moment in his kitchen when he had been about to kiss her. And she had wanted him to kiss her. In the dim light of the room, his cheeks were in shadow, his prominent cheekbones highlighted softly, his lashes dark smudges over his midnight eyes.

"Jennifer, I may know something about you," he said quietly, and as she gazed into his dark eyes, she felt as if she were about to step into a cavern filled with unknown terrors. A chilling premonition of disaster gripped her.

"From the tone of your voice, maybe I'm better off not knowing," she said, and the look he shot her confirmed her suspicions.

Three

———

Ben stood and walked to the window, gazing at the snow tumbling outside, his hands jammed into his pockets. She waited, yet with every second of silence, her dread increased.

When he turned around, his dark eyes sparked with anger that made something inside her want to throw her hands up and tell him to stop. Instead she waited quietly.

"When you tried to get out of bed, you said you had to find Ben Falcon. You were on your way to see me."

She frowned, staring at him. "You said we don't know each other."

"No, we don't, but I can make a guess why you were driving to meet me. I think my father sent you. He's hired you to get me to go home to work for him. He's done this before."

"Who is your father?"

"Weston Falcon. A few years ago he was a U.S. senator. He lives in Dallas and is CEO of Falcon Enterprises, which is primarily oil and cattle."

It sounded as though Ben was discussing a friend of his, yet Jennifer could hear the tight thread of anger in his voice. Feeling frustrated, she shook her head. "That means nothing to me. I don't remember."

Ben looked out the window again. "After you were admitted, I called him and got an answering machine. I left a message that you're in the hospital here. I called one of his employees and left the same message with him, so by tomorrow we should hear from my father. As soon as the storm abates, he'll send someone to pick you up."

Ben's broad shoulders were silhouetted against the snowy window and he looked solid and reassuring, yet she guessed there was a great deal he was leaving unsaid. When he turned around to look into her eyes, she became aware of his maleness, and she wondered about his effect on her. Was it because of her helplessness and his comfort? Or was it a sheer physical magnetism? He didn't seem happy with her, yet he had been kind to her, so the anger had to be bound up with his father.

"When daylight comes, I'm going home. You can wait here if you want—I'll take care of the bill. I know my father will send someone for you."

Panic gripped her and she knew it was unreasonable, but it was frightening to not be able to remember anything and to not know anyone.

He moved closer to the bed and looked down at her, touching her knuckles lightly with his fingertips. "Or if you'd feel better about it, I'll take you home with me until someone comes to get you."

She closed her eyes and caught his hand in hers. "Thank you," she whispered, feeling a surge of relief.

Ben experienced tiny sparks from her clasp. He looked at the top of her head, her shining hair. She seemed so vulnerable that sympathy rose inside him for her, yet he knew if she worked for Weston, she was tough and intelligent. He should walk out tonight, tell her goodbye and save himself some trouble. But he couldn't do it.

He went to sit down and she watched him, meeting his steady gaze. "I know I should stay here, but I feel more secure with you."

A strange humorless smile flitted across his face. He settled back on the chair. "You won't when your memory returns."

"You don't get along with your father."

He shook his head. "No, I don't. Weston is ruthless, determined and unrelenting. He's been incredibly successful in business, and he did it on his own. He came from a poor farm background. My grandmother was a Comanche, my grandfather had a tiny farm that finally failed. Weston has built an empire and he was determined that he would raise his sons to run parts of it exactly the way he had, only, neither of his sons were carbon copies of him."

"So, you have a brother?"

"He's deceased now. Geoff was younger. My mother was as strong-willed as Weston, fighting him to her last breath. When I was ten, she died in a car wreck. Weston said I inherited all her rebellion and wildness. My brother tried to be what Weston wanted, and failed. I fought him. He's never given up trying to get me back—using coercion, bribes, beautiful women—" He broke off when she frowned at the last.

"He couldn't have sent me as an enticement!" The words were out before she thought, and she blushed.

One dark brow arched and curiosity flared in his dark eyes. "Why not?"

Her cheeks burned, and she waved her hand, looking down at herself. "I guess I know that instinctively. I looked in a mirror here. I'm not the type of woman to be a—a physical inducement. I have freckles."

"You also have a body and you have this—" he said softly, leaning forward to stretch out a long arm and wind a lock of silky auburn hair around his fingers. She felt the gentle tug on her scalp as she looked into his dark eyes. He was leaning over the bed, only inches from her now. Her awareness of him intensified, startling her because she was having reactions that were strong. She decided it was because of her circumstances.

"I'm not fishing for compliments," she said, avoiding his steady gaze and feeling embarrassed by the conversation, yet certain he was wrong, "but I don't have the kind of body you're talking about. Thank you for your compliments though. And look—" She waved pale slender fingers at him.

He arched his brow again at her, catching her hand and glancing down at her small hand in his large, callused palm.

"Even if you ignore the cuts from the wreck, this doesn't look like the hand of a woman who would be a beautiful enticement," she said, too aware of the solid warmth of his hand holding hers. "Whatever work I do, I use my hands enough to prevent long, red nails. No, if you're right, he must have sent me to use my wits to talk you into coming home."

"That would be a first where a female is concerned," Ben replied dryly, leaning back against the chair, but still holding her hand, his thumb running idly across her knuckles. She wondered if he noticed what he was doing; she was too conscious of it. "And the most dangerous to me," he added softly with an arch of his eyebrow.

"I'm not a threat to you. I might not remember anything, but I know what my instinctive reactions are."

Suddenly his eyes twinkled as he gazed at her. "Stop arguing, Jennifer. I believe you."

"I'm glad you do." She studied him, wondering what he was like, what would make him laugh. "When did you leave Texas?"

"When I was twenty-six, eight years ago. The first time I left was when I was seventeen and ran away from home. After a couple of rebellious years, I decided to cooperate with him. I got a degree in petroleum engineering and went to work for him. Unfortunately, he wanted to make every major decision."

"You couldn't work any satisfactory agreement out between you?" she asked. Ben continued to rub his thumb across her knuckles, careful to avoid the cuts and bruises.

He shook his head, trying to bank the anger he felt as he remembered the struggle with Weston. "No, we couldn't. It was his way or no way."

"Maybe he was right. He was older and more successful."

Ben looked into her clear green eyes that appeared guileless and wondered how she had become entangled with Weston. She seemed intelligent and quietly self-possessed, not the type of woman he associated with his father. "My father was demanding and brutal when I was growing up. Geoff always conformed to save himself beatings, but he couldn't achieve the excellence my father demanded, so he paid a price emotionally.

"After I grew up a little, I finally decided that maybe I had been too bullheaded, that I should try Weston's way. When I got into the business, I found out things I had only suspected. My father places success first. He's not above hurting others, lying, cheating or anything he can do as long as it's within the law or he knows he won't get caught.

"It finally came to a takeover where he was going to crush good people to get a small company that would be a toy to him, something he'd discard as soon as he acquired it. I killed the deal and packed and left. I'm cut out of the will, and with Geoff gone, the fair-haired boy is Jordan Falcon, an older cousin who works for Weston." Ben shifted restlessly. "My cousin tries to be what Weston wants. They can have it all."

He became silent when a tall, white-uniformed nurse came to take Jennifer's blood pressure. As soon as the nurse left, Jennifer turned to him. "When did you move here?"

"I bought the ranch eight years ago. For the first four years Weston sent people to force me to come back. But the past few years, I haven't been bothered by him and I figured he had finally given up on me."

"Maybe you're wrong about me," she said quietly.

Studying her, Ben wished he were wrong, wished that she was trying to find him for an entirely different reason—one that had no connection to his father. He shook his head. "I don't think so, Jennifer."

"I might be related to someone who works for you and looking for him or her."

"No women work for me."

"I've talked too much. You're probably exhausted after working today in this storm. You don't have to stay awake."

"I'm all right and I'm glad to talk," he said, releasing her hand.

"I wish I could remember something. Do you think my purse was destroyed?"

He shrugged. "I'll go tomorrow and look for it, but it's probably blown to bits."

She shivered. "Thank heaven you found me."

"You would have probably survived on your own. You were struggling to get away from the car when I arrived."

She ran her hand across her head.

"Head hurt?"

"Yes, and I hope breakfast is at dawn because I could eat this bed, I'm so hungry."

"Why didn't you say so?" As he started to rise, she caught his hand.

"Sit down! It's the dead of night and I don't want you to go hunting down a candy machine—"

"I could use some food myself. He glanced at his watch. "There are all-night diners open around here—what's your choice?"

"Please don't go out in the storm for me."

"If you don't give me your choice, you'll have to take potluck," he said, aware she was still holding his wrist. She seemed to realize she was clinging to him and moved her hand to the bed.

"Now I feel terrible that you're going out in the storm."

"You'll be easier to feed than all those steers I have to take care of tomorrow." Her quick smile made him draw his breath. The dimple appeared in her cheek and he longed to really make her laugh.

"If you insist—" she began, big green eyes focused on him, "will you do one more thing before you go? Can you help me up? I want to get to the bathroom—" She was already pushing the covers away and swinging her long, shapely legs over the side of the bed. "I don't have any slippers and I have on this dreadful hospital gown."

"Come here," he said, lifting her into his arms. She wrapped her arm around his neck, her coppery hair spilling onto his shoulder. He was aware of the warmth of her body through the thin hospital gown and he was glad it was a short distance across the room because his body was reacting to her nearness. He stepped into the bathroom to set her on her feet, his hand brushing lightly across the bare backs of her thighs as he released her. She supported herself with a handrail, holding her injured ankle up. "Holler when you want my help," he said, stepping out and closing the door.

Feeling hot, too aware of each contact with her, he went into the hall and glanced up and down, his stomach growling in reminder that he hadn't eaten since breakfast. Spotting the lighted nurses' station, he walked down the hall and stopped in front of the desk. A nurse glanced up and then smiled.

"We're starving. Is there anything open near the hospital where I can get hamburgers?"

"Sure, across the street," she said, smoothing her blond hair.

"Is there anyplace I can get a magazine now? She asked for one."

"Here," she said, pulling magazines from beneath the counter. "And I'll check her in just a few minutes."

"Thanks," he said, giving her a broad smile, and she smiled in return.

He stepped back into Jennifer's room as she opened the bathroom door and started to hop out. He tossed the magazines and they landed at the foot of the bed. "I brought you some reading so you would stay awake. And none of that hopping around," he said, picking her up easily. He tried to focus on the bed to avoid looking at her, but he couldn't resist turning his head to gaze into her wide green eyes that were studying him with open curiosity.

"I don't know how you could have had such a dreadful time with your father—you're so cooperative. And if he's not, I don't know how I can work for him."

"Your memory will return and you'll get your answers," Ben said gruffly, barely aware of what he was saying, more aware of the soft womanly feel of her in his arms, her red lips only inches away, the thin hospital gown that was almost nothing. As he studied her, she blinked, her expression becoming solemn, her lips parting, and he wondered if she were having half the reaction that he was.

He bent down to place her on the bed, and when she lay back against the pillow, he wanted to follow her down, to feel her softness under the length of him, to pull away the flimsy hospital gown. He remembered the pink lace teddy, the triangle of auburn curls, and his body hardened in response. He gazed into green depths that seemed to tug on his senses with silent promises. With an effort he straightened up, looking down at her, unable to turn away because there was a chemistry generating between them that held him like a direct contact with an electric current.

"Ben," she said in the barest whisper, and his heart thudded against his ribs. He sat down on the bed beside her, his hip against hers while he leaned forward. He braced both hands on either side of her, bending close as she watched him, a slumberous invitation in her eyes until her dark lashes lowered.

He brushed his mouth over hers so lightly, the softness of her lips making him shudder. He wanted to tighten his arms around her, slide on top of her and kiss her passionately. Why was he having this reaction? Particularly with this woman who by tomorrow would be at cross-purposes with him? And then the thought was gone as her lips parted beneath his and he thrust his tongue over her full underlip, invading the velvety warmth of her mouth.

Jennifer moaned softly as he kissed her, his tongue going deep, touching the insides of her mouth and playing over her tongue. Her heart pounded violently while she returned his kiss, her tongue sliding into his mouth as she responded with an abandon that surprised her. An uncontrollable heat centered low in her body, spreading and making nerves raw, causing her to be conscious of the proximity of his strong male body.

He raised his head and she opened her eyes, looking into unfathomable darkness as he gazed solemnly down at her. Something flickered in the depths of his eyes and with a shock, she realized he looked angry.

"You're thinking about my working for your father."

"It's there between us," he answered, standing.

"Suppose you're wrong? Or suppose when I hear your side, I quit?"

Suddenly his features softened. "I'm blaming you for things that happened in the past," he said lightly, yet a muscle worked in his jaw. "I'll be back soon."

She watched him stride out of the room and lay back on the bed, wondering at the turn in her life.

Thirty minutes later Ben pushed open the door, and she dropped a magazine. Her heart jumped, her pulse accelerating because he strode across to the bed bringing with him a sense of strength and vitality that she needed. Snow was melting on his wide hat brim and across his broad shoulders, leaving sparkling drops of water in their place. Dropping sacks with mouth-watering smells of mustard and onions, he flung his coat and hat on a straight chair. Cold air swirled around him as he moved closer to help her get settled to eat.

He placed more packages on the bed. "I stopped at the hospital vending machine and bought you a comb, toothbrush, a few things. We're leaving in the morning before the stores open or I'd get you some other things."

"Thank you," she said, picking up the package with the comb and tearing it open to place it on the shelf beside the bed.

In minutes they were enjoying a feast of hamburgers and onion rings along with cans of cold cola. She closed her eyes as she chewed. "This tastes wonderful! Thank you."

"There are two burgers apiece."

She laughed, and Ben's heart thudded because the sound was as merry as the call of a meadowlark and her sparkling green eyes gave her a beauty that was breathtaking.

"I should have brought you *three* burgers and really made you laugh!"

"I can't possibly eat two of these giant burgers!"

He grinned at her and shrugged. "You said you were hungry. I'm hungry and I'll eat two."

"Yours goes to muscle. Mine would go to fat."

"There isn't an ounce of fat on your body," he drawled and watched her cheeks turn pink as she gazed at him. He shrugged. "I'd be abnormal if I hadn't noticed." He glanced through the window. "I heard the weather report while I was out. We're in for more snow, and parts of the state are losing power from frozen lines that are down.''

''You need to be home.''

''There isn't anything I can do tonight and in the morning, I'll be there. A chopper can get in and out.''

She sighed as she wiped her fingers and mouth and folded up the paper the hamburger had been wrapped in. ''What a feast! Thank you, Ben.''

He shrugged, starting on a second burger. ''I was starving, too.''

''Tell me more about your life.'' She sat up in bed and touched the back of his hand where a faint white line crossed from his knuckle to his wrist. ''How did you get hurt?''

''Canoeing long ago when I worked one summer on a ranch in Colorado. Turned over in white water and gashed my hand on a rock. I went to Texas University, was on the track team,'' he added between bites.

''You have a scar on your jaw.''

He looked amused as he touched the faint line across the lower part of his jaw. ''Horse kicked me—if it had been a little higher, I would have lost an ear. I ride in rodeos occasionally.''

''You weren't raised on a farm—why did you go into cattle and ranching?''

''Dad owns a ranch in West Texas and I used to spend summers there, and that was the best time of my life. I like engineering and I've worked on rigs and it's challenging, but when I left home, I wanted as far from the oil business as I could get. There's a satisfaction in living like I do. It's cussed mean at times like this,'' he said, glancing out the window where snowflakes still swirled and struck the glass to slide in a frozen heap at the bottom of the pane.

''This weather is bad for you and I've been so much trouble, but I feel safe in here, like I'm in a cocoon. I almost wish tomorrow wouldn't come. I feel shut away right now without any problems or past, but then there's no future, either.''

''You'll be all right, Jennifer,'' he said quietly and settled back in the chair, stretching out his long legs. ''With daylight your memory should return.''

She gazed into his dark eyes and felt a troubling uncertainty, yet his presence and the conviction in his voice were reassuring. Feeling as if she could talk to him all night, she leaned back against the pillow. ''You're not married?''

''No,'' he answered, shaking his head, his gaze going beyond her. ''Twice in my life I've been interested in a woman—one time it was on the verge of becoming serious, only I discovered she had been selected by my father.''

''Why would a woman do that?''

He gave her a cynical look. ''I'm healthy, sound in mind and body. Marry me with Weston's blessings and someday Falcon Enterprises would be mine and my wife's. Some women are willing to give that a try.''

She blushed. ''I didn't mean you wouldn't be appealing.''

''You didn't?'' he asked with great innocence, and she laughed again and he had to grin at her.

''I guess I'll find out a lot about you because all we can do is talk about you. I don't have anything to tell.''

He smiled, a quick smile that warmed her. ''You'll remember.''

''Tell me about getting started on your ranch.''

Locking his fingers behind his head, he told her about traveling cross-country and not intending to settle here, thinking he would go to Montana or Idaho.

It was hours later when his voice deepened, his words slowing. A nurse checked Jennifer often and had said it would be fine for her to sleep, yet they continued talking, Jennifer learning about Ben's ranch and life. Finally he dozed and she studied him, his thick lashes dark shadows on his prominent cheekbones, an air of strength about him even when he was asleep. With a sigh she closed her eyes and prayed that her memory would return with the dawn.

The next morning they boarded a chopper for home, Ben sitting beside Jennifer. She was pale and quiet, remembering no more than she had the night before. The snow had stopped, but more was predicted. As they flew in the first light of dawn, he held her hand in his. She looked solemn, as if she were headed for an ordeal, and he suspected she was worrying because her memory was still absent.

As the sun tilted over the horizon and the Sangre de Cristo Mountains loomed into view, snow sparkled on peaks. The dark horizon to the north was the only hint of the next storm brewing.

They set down and Ben jumped out, swinging her into his arms and striding to the house. Within minutes, Ben had Jennifer seated with her foot elevated and ice packs around it, he had placed a call to Zeb and built fires. He needed a shave and shower and he was hungry again, but he was paying for every second he had the chopper and he couldn't afford to wait. He rummaged in a closet and found crutches for her. As he pulled his coat on again, he faced her.

"Unless we run into trouble, I'll be back by midafternoon. You may get a call from my father, but I don't think anyone can pick you up unless he sends a chopper." His gaze ran over her ripped slacks and the green sweater. "I can't get to a store to get you other clothes, but you're welcome to my shirts or sweaters. They're in the bottom dresser drawer."

"Thanks." She nodded, using one crutch to follow him to the door. He paused as he looked down at her, thinking it seemed natural to have her in his house. He brushed a quick kiss on her forehead and strode outside.

Jennifer stood in the doorway, feeling the cold and watching the husky bound after the tall man. She felt as if Ben Falcon were her world, her family. Aware of a dull ache, she rubbed her hand across her head, gingerly touching the knot that was going down now.

Two men and a horse-drawn wagon had loaded square bales of hay into the chopper. Ben swung up into the chopper followed by another man, while the third one climbed into the wagon and turned toward the barn. In seconds the helicopter lifted and swooped out of sight.

She closed the door and then stood in the rustic kitchen, gazing at pine cabinets, fishing poles in the corner, the fire dancing on the hearth. The house was masculine and comfortable.

She hobbled into the living area, crossing to look at shelves with worn books—fiction and nonfiction, technical books on oil. She rubbed her head again, wishing memory would return, unable to believe that she could work for the monster Ben described. She moved closer to the shelves and a book caught her attention. The jacket was torn on a copy of Margaret Mitchell's *Gone With The Wind,* and Jennifer could remember lying on a rumpled fold-out bed and reading the novel. She remembered a crowded room with the Hide-A-Bed, the small house. Elation raced through her and she rubbed her head, straining to remember more, but nothing came. She replaced the book on the shelf, lightly touching it, wondering about the book's owner who seemed tough and so much an outdoorsman, yet who must like to read, as well.

Jennifer hobbled around the room to a table at one end of the sofa. She picked up a picture of a dark-skinned, dark-eyed young boy with black hair. His features didn't resemble Ben's and she wondered who he was.

Her gaze shifted to the phone and she almost dreaded hearing from Texas until she could remember everything. Right now she had to accept whatever people told her. She heard scratching at the door and limped across the room to open it. The husky trotted inside, leaving tiny puddles where his wet paws tracked as he passed her, going to his dog dish in the kitchen.

"Fella, you could at least wipe your paws before you come in."

By noon the sun was behind clouds and a howling wind was blowing over the mountain. Ben swung the hatchet and broke ice on the wide metal tank so the horses could drink. When he finished his task he climbed inside the Jeep. At the barn Zeb came striding into sight, waving his arm and Ben waited.

"Boss, I got a call from Derek. Their electricity is out and their generator is acting up."

"I'm on my way. Call and tell him, will you?"

"You're going to get caught in the storm."

"I'll call if I need help."

"What about the woman?" Zeb asked, glancing toward the house.

"She'll be all right. Zeb, I think Weston sent her."

The short, wiry man frowned, rubbing his thin red nose with a gloved hand. "She doesn't remember anything?"

"Not yet, but she told me she had to find Ben Falcon. There's only one reason she would be on that errand. I called Weston, so when the storm lets up, he'll probably send someone for her."

"We letting them on the place?"

"Sure, as long as all they do is get her and go."

"Want me to check on her?"

Ben glanced at the house and shook his head. "You don't need to. She's not that injured. I'll be back before long, I hope." He shifted and drove away, passing the house and heading down the mountain to the highway to drive to the boys' ranch.

As he passed beneath the iron arch that read Bar-B Ranch, he thought about the boys he had met at the ranch, some teens, some tiny little kids. The ranch provided a good home for them and Ben tried to support and help any way he could. Since all the money he made had to be plowed back into the ranch, he gave his time and any expertise he might have. Each spring he gave the ranch a new foal and four calves, and this year he hoped he could do more.

When he slowed behind the rambling structure that was home for the director, his assistant and the cook, as well as a dorm for the boys, Derek Hansen came out. He strode to the Jeep with Renzi trudging at his heels.

"Are we glad to see you!" Derek exclaimed.

"I don't know if I can fix anything or not."

"You'll do better than we can. Jerry and I are all thumbs when it comes to machines, and the only kid with a mechanical bent has been working on the generator for over an hour now."

Ben jumped down and pulled a tool chest from the back of the Jeep. He hunkered down in the snow to be on eye level with the five-year-old. Big, brown eyes stared at him.

"Renzi, you shouldn't be out here. It's cold."

"Yes, sir. You and me will build a snowman."

"Not in this blizzard."

"Yes, sir. When you fix the generator, we'll build a snowman," he pronounced solemnly.

Ben grinned and squeezed Lorenzo's shoulder. "All right. One little snowman if my fingers aren't freezing."

Lorenzo bounded away, running in circles in the snow, and Derek shrugged. "He's been asking all day when you were coming."

"Heard anything from his mother?"

"She's still thinking about giving him up. She's dating and she doesn't want Lorenzo." Ben felt a stab of pain as he watched Lorenzo making tracks in the snow.

"Dammit, I want him to know someone wants him."

"I can't tell him you do because at this point in his life he might prefer you and he's not going to have a choice."

"The minute she says she's giving him up, I want to start the paperwork for adoption."

Derek glanced at Ben, and Ben met his gaze as wind whipped against him. "Raising a kid is trouble."

"I know that, and in some ways I feel damned incompetent, but I've been around him enough that I can trust myself not to be the bastard my father was."

"I never had a worry about that. For over six years you've given us a lot of your time and you're more patient with these kids than Jerry and I—and we're trained and dedicated. God knows, you have to be dedicated," he said, striding across the snowy yard to a metal shed. Lorenzo raced after them and followed them inside where a slender, black-haired sixteen-year-old boy with his face smudged in grease, looked up at them.

"Hi, Mr. Falcon."

"Ben, you remember Todd Gibson," Derek said as Ben smiled.

"Hi, Todd. You were the one who wanted to ride the bull in the rodeo."

Todd grinned. "Yep, and next time I will."

"Let's look at this," Ben said, bending over the machine that had been patched and wired. In seconds he was lost in thought about the generator while Todd passed him tools and Lorenzo sat on the floor and poked through his toolbox, finding a measuring tape to play with. Ben never even noticed when Derek left.

Finally Ben stepped back. "Hit the switch."

Todd thrust out fingers blackened by grease and touched the switch. The generator cranked to life and a light came on overhead.

"That's great, Ben!" Todd exclaimed.

"Yeah, well, you helped, too. Let's hope it works until the electricity comes on again."

"They said wires are down."

Ben gathered his tools while Todd bent over to help. Ben glanced at him, remembering when he was Todd's age, wishing he had had a place like the ranch that would have been a haven and a far better family than the one he had.

"Are we going to build a snowman now?" Lorenzo asked, planting his sturdy legs in front of Ben.

"Sure. One quick snowman."

"Not me!" Todd exclaimed. "I'm frozen."

Ben picked up his coat, Todd and Lorenzo following while Ben closed the door behind them and they crossed the yard. The gray sky was spitting sleet and snow, and a gust of wind whipped bits of ice against Ben's cheek as he leaned forward. He placed the tool chest in the Jeep. "Lorenzo, this snow is too flaky and dry for a snowman."

"You can do it, Ben," Lorenzo declared firmly.

Ben shook his head as he knelt to scrape snow into a heap. It was too cold to pack easily, but after a few minutes, he had one large ball and was working on another. Finally he held Lorenzo up to let him place two rocks for eyes, another rock for a nose and a twiggy mouth. Lorenzo stepped back to admire their work.

"See! I knew you could make a snowman."

"You did it, too, Renzi. Now let's get inside and warm up." He strode to the back door with the child running beside him.

Stomping snow off their boots on the porch, they stepped into a kitchen filled with the tempting smell of stew cooking on a large gas range.

"I was going to get you," Derek said, handing a mug of steaming coffee to Ben. "Thanks a million for coming to our rescue."

"Todd about had it," Ben said, taking the hot mug in his hands and sipping. "I need to wash up and get going—"

"Stay and eat with us."

"Sorry, not tonight. From what I've heard, we have another big storm headed our way. I want to get home."

Lorenzo had pulled off his wet coat and he stood in front of Ben, his eyes shining with pleasure. "Thank you for building the snowman. I can see him from the window. And I have the first snowman here."

Ben knelt down to give him a hug and then he stepped back. "It was fun, Renzi. Now you get out of your wet boots."

"Yes, sir."

Ben washed and went back to sit a few minutes and drink the coffee. As soon as he finished, he pulled on his coat. When he left, Derek walked to the car with him and offered his hand. "Thanks, again. Maybe next year we can buy a new generator. By the way, are your animals okay?"

"Yes. We got food out to them today. How about yours?"

Derek gazed past him as snowflakes tumbled on his bare head. "The older boys do a good job when we get in a situation like this. We have a good bunch right now."

"You usually do." Ben swung up into the Jeep. "Pray for spring." He started the motor as Derek jogged back to the house. Ben glanced in the rearview mirror at the little snowman with a lopsided grin, snow swirling around it. If Renzi's mother didn't want him, Ben wanted to adopt him. The child was loving and trusting—he would be cared for at the ranch, but Ben wanted the boy to have a home of his own. Ben shifted his attention to the road.

A howling blizzard was setting in, and Ben sat hunched over the wheel until he turned onto his private road. Instead of following it up the mountain, he shifted and took the road to the valley and the creek. There was still enough light to see and he was curious about Jennifer.

He drove along the valley and parked, climbing out near the blackened wreckage of her car. He walked through the debris, kicking over a piece of metal. He bent down to turn the metal in his hands. It was the license plate, and while it was charred and muddy, he could see that it was a Texas plate, confirming his guess about where she had come from.

He poked through bits and pieces of the car, finding only charred scraps, until yards from the wreckage he picked up part of a purse. It was a billfold, burned into cinders that crumbled in his hand, except for a couple of hard objects. He pulled out melted, blackened plastic cards that were almost unreadable with only a barely discernible name. Ben ran his thumb over the raised letters as snowflakes fell on the charred plastic.

Jennifer Osmann Falcon.

Ashes mixed with snowflakes as they drifted to the ground while he turned in long angry strides back to the Jeep.

Four

Ben jammed his foot on the accelerator, spinning snow out behind the wheels as he headed back toward the road. When he reached the winding road, he slowed, driving with care while his thoughts churned. *He had Weston's wife at his place!*

Jennifer Falcon. He had heard when his father remarried, but it had been the year he had left Texas and he didn't remember her name. Jennifer had to have been a child bride because she looked as if she had to have been about fifteen years old eight years ago.

Unless this was Weston's *third* wife. Ben wouldn't have known about a third marriage since he had severed all contact with Weston and his people for the past four years. Ben felt waves of anger rising in him and he knew it wasn't just because Weston's wife had come to try to talk him into returning. He was enraged because he wanted her.

"Dammit," he muttered, gripping the steering wheel so tightly, his fingers ached because he could remember in the finest detail how it had been to kiss her. "Damn you, Weston," he swore, peering at the snow and knowing no one could get in to pick her up. Why had Weston stooped to sending his wife?

Unless perhaps Weston was ill? Ben rejected that thought as he pictured his tall, powerful father who at six feet four inches was an inch taller than Ben and forty pounds heavier—though the weight was all muscle. Weston worked out when he was in Dallas and rode all day when he was at the ranch. Ben couldn't picture illness interfering in Weston's life. So why had Weston sent his beautiful, young wife? The only answers made Ben's stomach knot. And she wasn't wearing a wedding ring—Weston would have given her one as ostentatious as a headlight. Why had she removed it? The reasons that came fueled his rage.

The ride seemed an eternity. When Ben finally strode from the garage to the house, he stared at the lighted windows, each rectangle a pale yellow glow muted by snowflakes, his thoughts still churning that Weston's wife was inside. Unaware of sleet pelting his jaw, he strode through the kitchen door, Fella dashing in with him before Ben slammed the door shut.

Jennifer's head jerked around, her auburn hair swirling across her shoulders. She stood beside the stove, a large spoon in her hand, an enticing aroma of chili filling the kitchen. The green sweater she wore made her eyes a deeper color, reminding him fleetingly of emeralds. And as his gaze ran over her swiftly, he pictured the pink teddy beneath the sweater and torn slacks. His gaze snapped back up to lock with hers. Her eyes widened as she stared at him, and he clenched his fists.

Rage made him shake. While he crossed the room in long strides, she frowned, placing the spoon on the counter.

"What's wrong?"

He caught her arms. "Has your memory returned yet?" he asked, the words grating, his voice deep from anger.

"No, it hasn't. Let go of me," she said firmly, staring at him.

Her eyes were wide, looking so innocent and guileless, as if there were no ulterior motives in her being at his house. She faced him steadily, curiosity and defiance obvious in her expression.

He inhaled deeply and released her. She didn't remember anything, and if he yelled at her, it would be like yelling at his husky. She didn't remember she was Weston's wife. Ben yanked out the credit card and held it in front of her.

When she glanced at it, her brows drew together in a frown. Taking the card from him, she stared at it, and he clenched his fists and turned to cross the room to stare out the window. He didn't dare stand close to her because he wanted to touch her. He inhaled and cursed Weston silently.

"You found this at the car?"

"Yes. It seems you're his wife."

Silence filled the room and when Ben felt he had his emotions more under control, he turned to look at her. She was still frowning, staring at the card. She ran her hand over her forehead.

"I don't remember," she said so softly and looked up at him, a stricken look in her eyes. "I don't remember a husband or a man named Weston. I just don't remember."

"It'll come to you. I'm surprised he hasn't called."

"The phone is down. You had a call from a man named Horace Williams about some horses, but we were cut off and it hasn't been working since."

"It probably doesn't matter. If Weston sent you here with a goal in mind, he may not be so quick to come get you, anyway," Ben said, clenching his fists and wondering about her.

Jennifer stared at Ben and he drew another deep breath, feeling a wrenching in his middle because he wanted to cross the room to her and she was as forbidden to him as poison.

She blinked and looked down at the card again, shaking her head.

"I'll clean up and be back," he said tersely.

"Dinner's ready. I hope you like chili," she remarked, but he wondered whether she knew what she was saying to him because she was still studying the card in her hand.

He yanked off his coat and hat and draped them on pegs by the door and turned to her, his hands on his hips. "Get off your foot. I can fix the damned dinner."

When she raised her chin, he felt the tension snap between them. "I can manage," she said quietly in a firm voice and turned her back to him. She picked up the spoon to stir the chili and then replaced the spoon on the counter. His gaze ran down her back over the sweater and torn slacks and for an instant again he mentally whisked away the woolen garments, envisioning her in the pink teddy, remembering her long legs and soft curves.

She moved awkwardly to the sink and he felt his temper rise because she didn't need to be hobbling around. The table was set for two and he could imagine how much time and effort it had taken with her bad foot. As she reached high in the cabinet for a serving bowl, he clamped his jaw closed tightly, fighting the impulse to pick her up and carry her out of the room and tell her to leave everything to him. Abruptly he turned and left the room.

Jennifer looked over her shoulder to watch him go, seeing his long, angry strides, knowing he was trying to control his temper. She glanced down at the card again and fear gripped her. She didn't remember a husband. And she had liked Ben's kisses. She was Jennifer Osmann Falcon—married to Ben's father! When she tried to think of Weston, she was blank. Closing her eyes, she prayed her memory would return. She rubbed her head and placed the burned card on the counter, turning to wash her hands and get a package of yellow corn tortillas from the fridge.

She worked slowly, getting water and ice in the glasses, stirring the chili again, checking on a frozen cobbler she had placed in the oven to bake.

She was putting the chili and tossed green salad on the table when she heard the scrape of Ben's boots as he crossed the living area to the kitchen. When he stepped into the room, her pulse jumped because his presence was as jolting as an electrical current. His neatly combed raven hair was damp, clinging to his neck, and he wore a fresh blue chambray shirt and faded jeans that clung to his narrow hips. His dark-eyed gaze stabbed at her and she felt his anger as tangible as the heat radiating from the stove.

"You sit down and I'll serve dinner," he said, crossing the room and taking the plate of salad from her. His fingers brushed hers, and he stood close enough that she could catch the clean scent of him.

"There's no need to treat me like an invalid," she said, wondering if she felt a need to defy him because of his anger toward her.

She tried to reach past him to place the salsa on the table, but as she turned to avoid touching him, she bumped a chair and it caused her to lose her balance slightly. She moved the crutch to keep from falling, but even as she steadied herself, Ben's arm circled her firmly and he took the crutch from her. Without a word, he set the salsa on the table and then he scooped her up and hooked his toe around the leg of the kitchen chair to pull it out. He set her down, releasing her instantly as if he had picked up a burning skillet. Embarrassed, too intensely aware of the moment in his arms, she waited in silence while he served dinner.

As they began to eat, Jennifer noticed he was staring out the window, his features looking hard and inscrutable, and she could feel the invisible barrier between them. Was he worrying about his livestock, or still mulling over his discovery about her identity? "Did you get your cattle fed?"

"Yes. It's late in the spring for a storm like this and hopefully it'll end tonight and the thaw will come soon." His gaze swung around to hers as he waved his fork. "Thanks for fixing dinner," he said.

She nodded. "You like this kind of life? You said you're an engineer."

"Yes, I like it here. It's a daily challenge and I work for myself. I like the land and the freedom and the peace here. I'll never go back."

Jennifer wondered about his solitary life. Was there a woman? She glanced at him over the rim of her water glass and felt certain there was one. He was too attractive and sexy to live the life of a hermit. He looked up from eating, his smoldering gaze meeting hers and she felt caught, unable to glance away. Jennifer's world narrowed down to his dark eyes, and she lost awareness of all else.

"I can't imagine why he would send you," he said gruffly.

"I can't imagine that I'm married." With an effort she tore her gaze from Ben's. "It's like being in a vacuum. I have nothing to base decisions on, nowhere to turn." She looked at him. "Thank you for bringing me back here, because whether you like it or not, you're the only certainty in my life."

He arched a brow, giving her a sardonic look. "Well, I'm a damned hostile one. If you're his wife, you're part of Weston."

"Right now he doesn't even exist for me," she said, feeling as if she were caught in a raging storm with no shelter.

"Only for a day or two. You won't be in a vacuum when Weston gets you. You'll be surrounded by servants and employees and he'll get the best medical care for you."

She looked down at her hand and waved her fingers at him. "Why don't I have a wedding ring?"

His thick lashes lowered as he looked at her hand and reached out to take it, running his thumb across her knuckles. The touch was so slight, yet it sent tingles spinning in her. He dropped her hand as if he realized what he had just done, and his gaze met hers. A muscle worked in his jaw while he studied her.

"You must have taken it off as you drove up here," he said, his voice laced with cynicism. Ben felt anger stir again as he thought about her lack of a ring. He could see the perplexity in her gaze, but he could imagine Weston talking her into doing most anything to achieve his purpose. "Maybe you didn't want me to know you're his wife for a while."

"Why would I—" She broke off, staring at him, her brows drawing together as she frowned. "I told you before, I'm certain I'm not the kind of woman someone would use to tempt a man. And if I'm married, I'd never do that!"

Ben wondered if she had the faintest idea how aroused she could get him by just a toss of her head.

"We won't know until your memory returns. Except I know Weston and what he's capable of doing." She was glaring at him now, bristling like a hound confronted by a bear. And in spite of what he suspected and all the antagonism between them, Ben still found her incredibly desirable. "You're not eating," he observed.

When she shook her head without answering, he wondered if he had pushed too hard. "Dammit," he said softly. He shoved back his chair and went around to pick her up and carry her to the living area. He was too aware of the soft weight of her in his arms, her curves pressing against him, her arm around his neck. She smelled soapy and sweet, her hair tickling his jaw, and his body was responding to her. He placed her on the sofa and moved away to stack another log on the fire.

"Whatever your motives for being here or for taking off your wedding ring, I keep reminding myself that right now you're innocent of them," he said brusquely.

She pinched the bridge of her nose. Suddenly her head jerked up. "There's a cobbler in the oven. It'll burn—"

He strode out of the room and in minutes she heard him cleaning the kitchen. She settled against the sofa, dismayed to think that might be her stepson in the kitchen and that she was having an intense physical reaction to his mere presence. As memories of his kiss returned, she shifted angrily, trying to shut out the recollection.

"Care for cobbler and ice cream?" he asked from the doorway. She hadn't heard him leave the kitchen and he stood with his sleeves rolled back, his hands on his hips as he studied her. She wondered how long he had been standing there.

"I'm not that hungry," she answered quietly.

He rubbed the back of his neck. "Look, you haven't eaten enough—"

"I'm all right," she said, longing for the quiet moments of closeness she had shared with him at the hospital last night when he had seemed to lose all hostility. As he shrugged and disappeared back into the kitchen, the lights blinked.

Minutes later when he reappeared, the lights flickered again. He placed the crutch near the sofa and crossed the room. The husky followed at his heels and curled up in front of the fire. Ben's shirtsleeves were still turned back; a flat watch with a leather band was on his left wrist. The watch looked businesslike, and his hands and wrists were strong and masculine, giving him an aura of quiet competence. Why was everything about him heightened, more memorable, more noticeable?

"The lines are coated with ice and we have a slight wind. We may lose electricity." He picked up the phone, listened a few seconds and replaced the receiver. "The phone is still out."

The lights blinked again and went off. The room was illuminated in a rosy glow by the blaze in the fireplace, leaving the corners in dark shadows. Ben crossed the room to sit down on a navy leather wing chair and remove his boots. He was close to the fire, the dancing flames casting an orange glow that highlighted his strong cheekbones, emphasizing his rugged handsomeness. Jennifer felt a pang of longing because the moment could have been so different. Her gaze ran down the length of him, over his long legs and then she turned away swiftly, reminding herself that she had a husband in Texas.

"I have only one bedroom, so you take the bed and I'll sleep in here."

"Of course not," she answered. "You keep—"

His head swung around, his gaze locking with hers again. "Let's not argue. You're hurt and you can have the bedroom."

"Do you want me to go into the other room so you can be alone?" she asked bluntly. It was only a little after eight and she was far from feeling as if she would go to sleep, but she wondered if her mere presence irritated him.

As Ben studied her, his pulse accelerated. He knew she had no idea how seductive she appeared. The subdued light from the fire made her look more accessible and hid the coolness in her gaze. Her hair was a silky curtain falling over her shoulders. With her shoes kicked off, her feet on the sofa, she had twisted around, stretching her leg out, her other leg bent at the knee. "Not unless you want to leave," he answered, conscious that his voice had thickened. He damned Weston again for getting him into this situation. He felt as if he were sitting in a mine field, on the verge of making a disastrous move.

"You said last night that you've never been married. Who's the little boy?" she asked, pointing to the picture on the table at the foot of the sofa.

"That's Renzi, one of the kids on the ranch."

"I remember you telling me about the ranch. Why do you have this particular little boy's picture?" she persisted.

"He's special," Ben replied, his voice changing. Jennifer felt an unexpected yearning because his voice filled with tenderness, a tone he had used a few times with her. Was she so susceptible to the slightest thing about Ben because of her vulnerability?

"Is he an orphan?" she continued, wondering if Ben would rather she kept quiet and left him alone.

"No, he's not. Most of the boys have families but for some reason the families can't take care of them. Renzi's mother is getting a divorce and she has legal custody, but right now she can't afford to keep him." Ben rubbed the back of his neck. "I don't think his mother wants him."

Jennifer detected the bitterness in his voice and she glanced at the picture, feeling a pang for the child. "Can't he stay at the ranch? Is there an age limit?"

"Boys can stay until they're eighteen, so he'll have a home. His mother is on the verge of placing him up for adoption and if she does, I've thought of applying to adopt him."

"You sound uncertain about it," she said, curious because he sounded so sure about everything else.

He sat in silence for a moment as if he were debating whether to discuss it with her. "I'd like to take him, but I'm not certain what kind of father I'd be. I didn't grow up with a good example."

"Are you scared you'll be like your father?"

"Yes." She realized she had struck a nerve. "You wouldn't be," she stated matter-of-factly. "You're furious with your father and with me. Yet even under trying circumstances, you've been nothing but kind to me, so I'm sure you'd be good with a child. Especially one you love."

He rubbed the back of his neck again and stared at the dancing flames. "Sometimes I'm not sure that I'd know how to handle difficult situations with a little kid."

"I'd guess every parent feels uncertainty like that at one time or another. I'm sure you'd be a good father," she said and he looked at her, his features softening momentarily.

He gave her a crooked grin and she felt a rush of warmth. "You barely know me." He shifted and stretched his long legs toward the fire, wriggling his toes. "I give my Sundays to the boys and try to spend time with them or fix things over there—help any way I'm needed. I started this ranch on my savings, but the amount was a shoestring. I keep pouring everything back into the place, so I try to give my time to the boys' ranch. That's how I've gotten to know Renzi so well."

"Is the boys' ranch your neighbor?"

"Yes, to the north. I've been buying land to the west. I'll buy it wherever it's available. My herd gets larger each year." He talked quietly and she listened, hearing the anger leave his voice and the friendliness return. They talked about the ranch and the boys until she saw that it was past one o'clock in the morning. The lights had come back on over an hour ago.

"Good heavens! I didn't realize the time, and you've worked outside in this storm all day. You can't go to bed until I get out of here," she said, struggling to stand.

Ben stood and fought the urge to cross the room and pick her up and carry her to the bedroom. She was Weston's wife! He knew the hour was late, but he enjoyed talking to her.

"Towels are in the bathroom cabinet," he said. "You can have the bathroom first. Sorry there's only one, but this is a small place."

"Not so small really," she said, flashing him a smile, and then growing somber. "Good night, Ben."

"'Night," he said, watching her slow progress, knowing his area rugs made it more difficult for her. He crossed the room to let the husky outside, feeling the draft of cold lash him. The sleet and snow had stopped and the ground sparkled. Ice crackled slightly as a wind blew across the mountain and limbs sparkled in the moonlight. The world looked pure and untouched.

Ben closed the door, picked up dishes and rinsed them, then let the dog in. The husky bounded inside, running to his water bowl to lap before trotting to the bedroom to scratch on the closed door.

Ben switched off the kitchen lights and heard the husky. "Fella, c'mere," he ordered.

The husky ran to him and then back to the bedroom door to scratch. Jennifer opened the door and the husky ran inside.

"Fella!" Ben snapped.

"He's all right in here. I don't mind."

Ben barely heard her. She stood in one of his faded chambray work shirts, her long legs bare, socks on her feet. The shirt hung to midthigh and she looked incredibly sexy. Light behind her made a halo of fire of her hair and he could remember exactly how its silky texture felt. As if she became aware of his scrutiny, she touched the collar of the shirt, pulling it closed beneath her chin. "You said I could use one of your shirts."

"I'm staring because I just haven't ever seen it look so good," he remarked in a deep voice. "Help yourself to whatever you want."

"While I'm still up, do you want to get your clothes for tomorrow?" Before he could answer, she continued, "I don't care if you want to come get them while I'm asleep in the morning. I'll be buried under covers."

"I'll do that," he said, knowing his voice had deepened again. He tried to avoid imagining her in bed, but failed completely as images taunted him of her sprawled on his big bed in only his shirt. "If the dog bothers you, toss him out. If I put him outside, he can get into the bunkhouse. They have a dog door."

"He's all right," she replied. Jennifer looked at Ben and he stared back, feeling tension coil between them. He wanted to move closer to her, to wrap his arms around her. Yet he reminded himself who she was and wondered how many times he would have to tell himself that she was his stepmother.

As soon as she closed the door, he moved restlessly around the room switching off lights, stripping off his shirt. He heard water running in the bathroom. He needed sleep, but he had a suspicion it wouldn't come easily.

Finally, the bathroom door opened and Jennifer faced him. "I'm going to bed now. The bathroom is yours."

"Sure." His gaze raked over her. Her face was scrubbed, the shirt unbuttoned far enough to reveal an enticing bit of flesh and soft curves.

She turned to hobble to the bedroom, his shirttail shifting over her round bottom with each step. He heard her close the door behind her. He jabbed a log, sending sparks spiraling up the blackened chimney, the smell of wood smoke filling the room. Ben fought images of Jennifer that wanted to crowd into his thoughts, and he silently cursed Weston again. He closed the screen, put away the poker and strode to the bathroom. The washed pink teddy hung over a rack and he drew a deep breath, picturing her in it while his hands moved over her sleek, warm body.

When the snow melted he was going to town and find a woman. He had been isolated out in the wilds too long and was having a reaction to Jennifer that he hadn't experienced since he was eighteen years old. It was unreasonable, consuming. When he had dated Andrea Murdock, he had never had this compelling reaction or fiery awareness. He brushed his teeth, trying to ignore the pink teddy, but aware of it in his peripheral vision. And then the images returned of Jennifer in his bed, wearing only his shirt, her long, shapely legs bare.

He slammed the cabinet, shutting the door on his hand. "Dammit!" This time he swore aloud and didn't care whether she heard him or not.

In minutes he stripped to his briefs and wrapped himself in a comforter on the sofa, stretching out and watching flames dance in the fireplace. He shifted his thoughts to Renzi, wondering what it would be like to have full responsibility for a child.

As the fire turned to smoldering embers, Ben placed another log on the fire. He poked it grimly, knowing he should sleep, yet his restless body was in torment as erotic images of Jennifer still plagued him. He crawled back beneath the comforter and finally oblivion came.

Two hours later a scrape brought his eyes open. He heard another sound and stared into the darkness until he heard the back door close. Frowning, he stood and saw Jennifer outlined against the window as she tried to move through the darkened room.

"Jennifer—"

As he said her name, she bumped a table. Afraid she would fall, he rushed across the room and reached out to steady her, his hand resting momentarily on her waist, feeling the curve of her hip.

"Your dog wanted out," she said breathlessly. "I was trying to avoid waking you."

Ben yanked his hands away from her, too aware she wore nothing beneath the shirt.

"At least turn on a light so you can see where the hell you're going," he said, reaching to switch on a lamp.

Soft light came on, and Jennifer blinked while he straightened up. He wore only his briefs, and she was mesmerized, her gaze drifting over him, looking at his lean hard body that rippled with muscle as he moved. His shoulder was cut and had a dark bruise. She inhaled and glanced away, her cheeks burning.

"Sorry," he said, "I forgot my undress. Go on to bed. I'll get the light."

"Your dog will want back in," she said, avoiding looking at him, yet too aware of him standing so close.

"I'll let him in," Ben said in a tense voice. While he moved away, she glanced at him and then wished she hadn't because when her gaze met his, she felt unable to look away, tension and attraction crackling between them. Only, this time, every nerve in her body was raw from her awareness of his bare body and his tight briefs.

With an effort she turned and moved toward the bedroom, her back tingling because she guessed he was waiting and watching her. She closed the door and leaned against it, feeling drained because each encounter with him was volatile. She looked at the rumpled big bed, remembering his whipcord length and mentally picturing him on the bed. She felt shaky and exhausted as if she had walked a mile instead of across the house. She hobbled to the bed and sank down, looking around her, thinking the room was a reflection of its owner with its bookshelves and gun rack and wide mahogany desk and fireplace. She stretched out, wondering if she would be awake the rest of the night.

Lying on the sofa again, Ben shifted restlessly. He had been so scared she was going to fall and get hurt again that he had forgotten his appearance until the moment he switched on the light, and then it had been too late. He swore under his breath and turned to stare through the frosted window and the white world outside. How long would the snow last? How long before Weston would come get his wife?

Before dawn the next morning, Ben rose and crossed the room and rapped lightly on the bedroom door. When there was no answer, he opened it carefully. Jennifer was snuggled in bed, her hair spread across the pillow and blanket. Ben tiptoed to the bed to look down at her. Only her eyes and nose and the top of her head were visible. She had the covers pulled high, her lashes dark on her cheeks as she lay turned slightly on her side and curled up. Ben felt his body responding to the sight of her because she looked warm, accessible.

He turned and tiptoed across the room to get fresh clothing, and then with one last glance at her, he closed the door and moved across his house to get breakfast.

Jennifer stirred and came awake slowly. She turned her head and gazed at a gun rack. She felt disoriented, confused. Where was she? This wasn't her room with its pale blue-and-silver wallpaper, the white wicker furniture. She glanced out a window that was framed in snow. And then she remembered the previous night and Ben. She was in Ben Falcon's bedroom. Weston had sent her to Colorado to talk Ben into coming back home to work at Falcon Enterprises. She sat up in bed and remembered the blizzard while driving in the mountains. Jennifer blinked, suddenly holding her head. Weston had sent her here to talk to Ben. *She remembered!*

Thoughts and memories swirled in her mind—her childhood of poverty because her father gambled everything he made, her father's death, the men in her mother's life until she met Weston, the change in their lives when her mother married Weston, the luxuries, the ease, college—Devin Coleman. Devin.

Frowning, Jennifer recalled falling in love with Devin when she was a junior and he was a graduate student in physics and they had planned to marry. She recalled the times she told him she wanted to be so very certain before they lived together and his agreeing—and the moment she found the note in one of his texts from another woman. Jennifer remembered it all, recalling the confrontation with Devin, hearing the words that cut so deep. Devin had faced her in her apartment, his hands on his hips, locks of brown hair falling across his forehead as his blue eyes gazed at her angrily. "You belong in accounting. You're uptight and frigid. I found someone else, Jennifer."

While Jennifer pushed out of mind the memory that still stung, she wrapped her arms around herself and thought about Weston, his heart attack, his wanting Ben back and

Jordan trying to talk him out of it. Jordan Falcon, the nephew whom she tried to treat with courtesy, making an effort to curb the dislike she felt for him.

Throwing back the covers, she reached for the crutch, her heart pounding as she climbed out of bed and hobbled to the door. She remembered the drive from Dallas. She remembered all of it—

"Ben! Ben!" she cried, her heart pounding with excitement as she opened the bedroom door and stepped into the living area. "Ben!" she exclaimed with joyous relief.

He appeared from the kitchen. He was bare-chested, in jeans with the top button still undone, his hair tangled, and he was barefoot. His brows drew together in a frown. "What's wrong?"

"Ben, I remember!" she exclaimed exultantly, feeling as if weights had lifted from her shoulders. "I remember who I am and why I'm here. I remember it all!"

"I'm glad," he said solemnly, studying her, his gaze moving over her, and suddenly she realized she was still wearing only his shirt. She held the collar closed beneath her chin as she stared at him.

"Ben—" He met her gaze, and she felt her pulse race. "I'm not Weston's wife. I'm his daughter."

Five

————

Ben's eyes narrowed as he stared at her in shock. "You can't be!"

"I'm his adopted daughter," she said, her eyes sparkling. "Ben, I remember! I remember everything."

She laughed and the dimple showed; her teeth were white and even, and she looked joyous, exuberant and gorgeous. Ben wanted to laugh with her, but he couldn't because the damned ties to Weston stood between them like a towering barricade.

He stared at Jennifer without answering while he thought about Weston adopting her. It was something he couldn't imagine. Warmth and benevolence had never been a part of the father Ben had known. And beneath his surprise and curiosity was a swift rush of relief that Jennifer was not Weston's wife or blood daughter. As quickly as relief came, anger followed because Weston was using Jennifer to get him back to Texas. "I heard Weston remarried after I left."

"I know you were invited to the wedding. My father was Billy Osmann. He worked as a tool pusher for Falcon Enterprises and he died in an accident on a rig. When I was fifteen, Mother met Weston and married him and later he adopted me. My mother died four years ago."

At the time of the wedding, Ben remembered being mildly surprised that Weston was remarrying after so many years. At the moment, Ben was more curious about Jennifer.

"And you're not married."

"No, I'm not," she said, studying him, her smile fading. "That bothers you—why?"

He moved closer. "So Weston sent you here to talk me into coming back," he said quietly, knowing he sounded cynical and cold. But the only kind of woman who would be happy as Weston's adopted daughter would be a woman who loved money and power as much as Weston. And would overlook his lack of scruples.

"I don't see why that annoys you," Jennifer answered with a lift of her chin.

"I know my father and how his mind works. And what price he's often willing to pay to get what he wants." Ben felt anger filling him. Weston had sent Jennifer to get him back. What was she willing to do to talk him into it?

"I'll have to call him as soon as the phone works."

"You know he won't want you to come back until you accomplish what he sent you up here for."

Jennifer looked up at Ben, gazing into brown eyes that sparked with fiery anger and her joy was replaced swiftly by fury. She raised her chin and placed her hand on her hip, gripping the crutch tightly with the other hand and keeping her weight off her bad foot. "You listen to me, Ben Falcon. I don't know what kind of women he's sent after you before, but I'm not here to use my body to entice you back to Texas, and it's insulting for you to imply that I would. And it's absurd!"

"Absurd?" he said, grinding the word through his teeth and sounding dangerous. As if her words had goaded him to action, he stepped closer. His arm went around her, a strong band around her waist, a fierce bond that should antagonize her, but instead sent a flash of heat through her. "You're provocative, seductive—hell, I wouldn't expect you to announce you intended to seduce me into returning with you, but I know Weston. He didn't send you up here for a friendly chat!"

All her arguments vanished like mist in a wind. As his gaze dropped to her mouth, her heart thudded violently. She should push him away, refuse him, yet his words melted her resistance.... *Provocative...seductive.* The words tumbled in her mind because now she could remember the humiliation and hurt heaped on her by Devin's angry accusations, calling her frigid and cold.

Her lips parted, and she closed her eyes as Ben's head lowered. His mouth covered hers, his tongue sliding over her lower lip, invading her mouth, wet and hot and demanding. His arm tightened, pulling her against his hard length, and the image flashed in her mind of him as he had been last night in the briefs that hugged his trim hips and revealed his muscled body and powerful strength. While she slipped her arm around his neck, his arousal pressed against her, feeling rock hard, and insistent. Her resistance vanished. He made her feel seductive, desirable—a woman wanted by a strong man.

Ben's tongue thrust into her mouth, sliding over the velvety wetness of the inside of her lower lip, across her tongue and then her tongue went into his mouth, following his lead, inhibitions abandoned. He felt on fire, aroused, his emotions stormy. The inclination to protect her was gone now that she remembered fully why she was here. She had walked into the wolf's lair deliberately, so she took the risks and she could pay the price.

Bending over her, Ben tightened his arms angrily, shifting to slide his hand along her throat and then down to twist free the buttons on the chambray shirt. He pushed it open, his hand cupping her full breast. Heat spiraled down in him, throbbing and intense, making him ache. As she gasped, her hips thrust against him. She was hot and set him on fire with her eager response, and he intended to take whatever she wanted to offer. Her breast filled his hand, the softness and weight of it inflaming his need.

She moaned, twisting slightly so his hand brushed her nipple, and then he caught it between his fingers, rubbing it, listening to her gasp again before she kissed him wildly. He bent his head to take her nipple in his mouth, flicking his tongue over the taut bud as her fingers tangled in his hair. One arm still held her, but the other hand slid down, going beneath the shirt over her round, firm bottom. His hand slid over her thigh and slipped between her legs as he nudged her legs apart with his.

"Ben. Please—" As she gasped and twisted away, he stopped at once, raising his head to look at her.

Jennifer's heart thudded because he was a dangerous man who posed a threat to her peace. He was angry with her, taking what she would give, yet stirring her in a way no man ever had, which frightened her the most of all. She didn't want to be caught between two powerful men in a tug-of-war over their futures.

His eyes narrowed as he watched her, and she struggled to keep her gaze from drifting down to the bulge in his jeans.

"I have to stop," she continued. "I don't know you that well, and we've got enough turmoil between us already without complicating things." He gave her a cynical look. Did he think she was being coy or sly to win him over?

"You can't tell me you see my father as a kind person."

"I know he's manipulative and determined and ambitious," she admitted honestly. "I know he's accustomed to getting what he wants, but is his request so unreasonable?

You're struggling to make this ranch work. Look how difficult it is. You and your men had to battle the freezing weather—you've already lost cattle and maybe horses. You've lost money and had the expense of getting food to stranded cattle. You could go home to a job you're trained for and do well. You could take over a corporation that should give you all the challenges and satisfaction you want. Raising cattle is risky business."

"I'll have to hand it to Weston. He picks the best when he sends someone after me."

"He asked me to come talk to you. That's all!" she snapped, her green eyes filled with fire.

Yet he didn't believe her and he couldn't control his anger. He wound his fingers in her hair, turning her face up to his. "There was Andrea—her looks would melt all the snow on the ranch—and she offered everything if I would go back. Then he sent Madeline, who worked in a gallery in Taos. We had a brief friendship until I discovered she was sent up here on Weston's payroll. Their bodies were temptation and promises."

"I've already told you I'm not offering you my body!" she exclaimed.

"Why do I doubt that protest?" he replied, looking into the depths of her green eyes and thinking about her scalding response to him. "You said if Weston sent you, he sent you to use your wits to get me back. Well, I can believe that, too. And you're the most tempting woman there's ever been," he said in a harsh rasp, as if the words were torn from him. He bent his head, taking her mouth again in a savage, hard kiss, pulling her up against him.

Making him feel as if he were correct in all his assumptions, she melted against him, her hips thrusting against his in an instant, hot response that caused him to want to push her down on the floor and take her now.

He slid his hand between her bare thighs, touching her soft feminine folds, feeling the warm moistness that told

him how ready her body was. He touched the feminine bud
and heard her gasp and felt a tremor run through her. He
placed his palm against her, rubbing her, causing a friction
that drove her to a frenzy. Her fingers bit into him while her
hips moved swiftly. She moaned, her every twist and gasp
searing him.

Suddenly she broke away, falling against the wall. He
steadied her instantly, gazing into her eyes, his heart
pounding as violently as he had felt hers pounding.

"No!" she whispered, staring at him. "I didn't come to
offer my body to tempt you back to Texas. I can't be casual," she said, yet her cheeks flamed and her breathing was
ragged, and he suspected he could dissolve her resistance in
seconds. And he still didn't believe her denials, because he
had been taken in by Weston's women before.

He stretched out an arm, his hand resting on the wall beside her head, his body close in front of her, blocking her
from moving away. She inhaled, watching him warily.

"He's not paying me to bring you back."

"I find that damned hard to believe in light of past
events." Her green eyes were guileless, and Ben fought the
tendency to believe her and be taken in again, yet there was
a sweetness along with her fire that was incredibly convinc-
ing.

Ben moved away from her restlessly. "I don't know why
the hell I'm this important to him anymore."

"He had a heart attack last January."

Startled, Ben placed his hands on his hips. "How bad an
attack?"

"He's back at home and under a doctor's care, and Dr.
Gramercy, the family doctor, said he has to slow down. He
needs you to step in and take over."

"He has Jordan, who has wanted Falcon Enterprises
since he was seventeen years old. And I'm sure Jordan
didn't want you to come up here."

"No, he didn't. Sometimes I think Jordan causes trouble."

"Jordan has no scruples, but he always stays on Weston's good side. I've thought many times, it's a shame Jordan wasn't Weston's son."

"Weston doesn't want Jordan to take charge. He said you're the man for the job."

Ben swore, and her lips tightened. "Weston has never been willing to trust things to my judgment."

"He's not well and he needs you. When I go back to Texas, I'd like you to go with me," she said solemnly.

"No," he replied in an emphatic tone. "I'm not going back." Ben studied her, his anger still smoldering because he expected her to be clever. Weston wouldn't have adopted her if she hadn't been. And he didn't believe Weston was as sick as she was saying.

"You'll hear what I have to say, won't you?"

Ben kept reminding himself that while she sounded innocent and sincere, if Weston had sent her, she had to be as manipulative and deceitful as he was. Yet far more enticing. "I'll listen, but I'm not leaving my ranch. Even if I had to give all this up tomorrow, I wouldn't go back to work for Weston."

"Hear me out. He may have changed since you were there. I know you said you had trouble and you clashed—"

Ben felt a twinge of impatience with her. Looking at her hair that tumbled across her shoulders, he touched the corner of her mouth as if his hand were drawn to her against his will. Her lips were swollen and red from his kisses. Dropping his arm, he moved impatiently. "This is more than a clash," he stated quietly and turned around.

Jennifer looked at his muscled back that was laced with scars. She gasped in shock and then frowned. Ben turned around, and she knew the answer even though she still felt compelled to ask him. "Weston did that to you?"

"Yes, when I was a small child. He's abusive, determined to control everything concerned with his life. And if you know him, you have to know that."

"I told you that I know he's manipulative and wants his own way and he's impatient." She thought about the man who had become so important in her life. "He's never been cruel to me."

"Have you ever really clashed with him?"

She gave his question enough thought that he had an answer before she spoke. "No, I suppose not."

"The day you do," Ben stated quietly, "you'll see how ruthless he can be. He fought with my mother often. I can still remember their fights. And I don't believe a lion will turn into a tomcat." Ben moved closer to touch her hair, feeling its softness curl around his fingers. "So he sent you up here to coax me back," he said in a low voice. His emotions churned because he wanted her softness and her warmth. How long had it been since he had been touched and held? Or since he had held a woman? A damned long time now. He wanted Jennifer in his arms, her body against his, her long, slender arms around his neck. Yet at the same time, he knew she intended to elicit this reaction from him. Weston calculated each move, and he damned sure had calculated this one. The only unexpected turn had been the wreck and her amnesia. "You get dressed. I want you to go with me today."

"Where can we go? The roads will be impassable."

"Not for my Jeep. Just get dressed," he ordered, going to the kitchen. At the kitchen door he paused and glanced at her.

"Whatever argument we have between us, I'm damned glad you're not my stepmother." He turned around, disappearing into the kitchen.

Jennifer went into his bedroom and closed the door and felt as drained as she had the night before. Each encounter was more volatile than the one before. And all the coolness she had felt when she had been with other men, including Devin, that reserve that she had always experienced, vanished the moment Ben touched her. Never before had a man been able to turn her into a quivering mass of yearning flesh. He accused her of coming to the ranch to seduce him, but if anyone was guilty of seduction, it was Ben—even when most of his kisses had been out of anger. She drew a sharp breath. How could she resist him if he turned on his charm?

In thirty minutes she was showered and dressed in her torn slacks. She had found a thick navy sweatshirt of Ben's to wear. Enticing smells came from the kitchen and she entered to find he had cooked biscuits, grits and scrambled eggs.

He pulled out a chair for her, his gaze raking over her, the air sizzling again between them. As she sat down, his fingers brushed her shoulders so lightly, yet she felt his touch as if her skin had been bare.

"I helped myself to your sweatshirt."

"Looks better on you than on me," he said quietly as he set a chilled glass of orange juice in front of her and then poured steaming black coffee into a white china mug. He served them and she sat in silence, knowing that he wouldn't allow her to help.

When he sat down across from her, he gazed at her as he spread butter on a hot, flaky biscuit. "Tell me about Weston's attack."

"It happened on the golf course and they took him to the hospital in Dallas in an ambulance. They kept him for a week while he recuperated and they ran tests. Then, when they released him, he had another bunch of tests.

"Ben, your father has been good to me. When he met my mother, we were living in poverty. My memories of my real father are of a man who was lovable and totally unreliable. He drank too much and he was a compulsive gambler. I don't think my mother was always faithful to him, but he probably wasn't to her, either."

Ben drank hot black coffee and studied Jennifer. She had braided her thick hair and it hung in one long plait down her back. With her hair pulled back from her face, except for tendrils that escaped, her eyes looked larger than ever.

"Billy—that's all I ever called my father—gambled away everything he earned. We moved from oil field to oil field—he worked construction jobs. Mom was a waitress, sometimes a receptionist, a couple of times an exotic dancer because she said she made more money. But they fought over that and she stopped dancing. When I was fifteen, Billy died in the rig accident. He left tremendous gambling debts that Mom tried to pay off. During the day she worked as a receptionist and at night she worked as a waitress. I was in school and then worked in a grocery when school was out in the afternoon. Then she met Weston." Jennifer lowered the glass of orange juice and looked at him. "My mother was a very beautiful woman."

"I can believe that," he said easily, thinking she couldn't have been anymore beautiful than her daughter. Jennifer looked down and he didn't know whether she realized what he had meant or not. "What was her name?"

"Callie. She and Weston were married three months after they met. He paid off Billy's debts and moved us to Dallas and changed my life completely. I'd never had friends because of moving constantly. Suddenly I had a powerful, important stepfather who was a pillar in the community. He bought us clothes, he taught us how to move in society. When he married Mom, neither one of us knew which fork to use at a fancy dinner."

Jennifer's head was bent as she looked at her plate. Her voice was low, and Ben felt sympathy, but then realized she intended for him to feel sympathy for her. Weston had sent women who had tried sad stories on him before, stories that were no more true than Grimm's fables. Jennifer's might not be true, either, but right now he couldn't keep from believing her even though common sense urged him to keep up his guard.

"Weston's very good at taking people out of poverty and doing things for them to get them to do what he wants in return," Ben said, and her head raised, pinpricks of fire in her green eyes as she met his gaze steadfastly.

"You're a cynical man, Ben."

"I've learned the hard way." He pushed back his chair and picked up his plate. He looked at her half-touched food. "Finished?"

"Yes." She started to get up, but he took her plate.

"Sit down. Stay off your foot and let me do this."

"I work in accounting at Falcon Enterprises," she said, and he felt more certain her loyalty was with Weston.

As he moved around the kitchen, he caught her watching him several times. When he finished, he motioned to her. "Let's get our coats. Bundle up. I have a pair of moccasins you can wear so your foot won't get cold."

In minutes she was in the parka with gloves on her hands. He let the husky out the back door and swung Jennifer into his arms. "Leave the crutch. I'll stop by and get it as we drive past the house."

Jennifer wound an arm around his neck, intensely aware of his face only inches from hers, of his solid strength and strong arms around her. He pulled the door closed behind them and strode toward the garage with her in his arms, walking as easily as if he didn't hold her. He set her in the Jeep and in minutes they stopped while he got her crutch and closed the back door.

"You didn't lock your door."

"Who would be out here in this remote place?"

Shrugging, she wondered where they were going, riding in silence and looking at the sparkling white world. Sun shone brightly, ice glistening on branches and wires, snow coating dark limbs of the spruce, making them look like pictures on Christmas cards. The only sound was the motor of the Jeep. Snow flew up from the tires and she longed to get out and run across the untouched land.

"I wish I could walk in the snow. In Dallas we don't see much. I'd love to track in it."

He grinned at her, and she felt a clutch to her insides because when he smiled, he was irresistible. As his father could be, too. She knew at his charming best, Weston could win over most anyone to his views, and she wondered about the dark side to Weston, because the temper he had directed at Ben had never been turned on her.

Jennifer glanced at Ben's profile, seeing the strong jaw, the straight nose that added to his arrogant air, and she could imagine the two men clashing. She had seen Weston lose his temper, and he was fierce. Men at work scurried to please him and Jordan stayed out of his way, never crossing him. Many would call Jordan handsome, but she didn't like him, and her aversion to him colored the way she viewed him. He was devious, would lie to get what he wanted, always trying to please Weston. Weston was manipulative, but so was Jordan, and there were times she didn't think Weston realized how much Jordan influenced him.

They wound down the mountain on the snow-packed road and she found herself gripping the door handle. Ben glanced at her. "I'm not going to slide off the mountain."

She realized how tightly she was clinging to the door and she relaxed, releasing it and placing her hand in her lap as she looked at him. "I remember the wreck now. I was blinded by the snow and suddenly the car skidded and I lost control and then I went off the mountain."

"Don't think about it. It's over. You shouldn't have been driving in that storm."

"It wasn't that bad when I left the last town. Then when the storm intensified, it seemed worse to turn back than to go ahead. I didn't realize how mountainous it was going to get and how narrow the road to your ranch would be." He turned beneath tall trees and she frowned.

"Relax," he drawled. "I know these roads like I know the inside of my house. This is a shortcut over the mountain to the boys' ranch."

She sat back, trusting his self-assurance and his driving, enjoying the snowy world surrounding them. Near the top of the mountain the view became breathtaking. Below, she could see ponds with a wide stream connecting them. "You have a lot of ponds."

"I dammed up Flint Creek and that way I can control and conserve water for my livestock."

In minutes, they passed a ramshackle building of weathered boards; rusty mining cars were turned over on tracks that disappeared into the mountain.

"They say it's an old gold mine."

"You haven't looked for gold?"

He grinned, another irresistible smile as he shook his head. "I'm too busy looking for my cows."

As they wound down the mountain, she saw the corral and buildings of the boys' ranch. "Here's the Bar-B," Ben said.

"Do you need to see someone here?"

"They might need my help," he answered casually.

When they slowed at a cluster of buildings, three small boys came running toward them. As they clambered over him, Ben knelt to hug them while Jennifer climbed out, walking around the Jeep carefully, testing the snowy ground before she put her weight on the crutch. A blond boy glanced at Ben.

"Is this your girlfriend?" he asked in a squeaky voice.

Ben grinned and straightened up. "She's my stepsister," he said. "Jennifer, meet Johnny, Peter and Lorenzo. Guys, this is Miss Falcon."

"It's Jennifer," she said, shaking hands with each boy as she shifted her weight and leaned more on the crutch.

"We're making a snow fort. Come help us, Ben," Renzi urged, tugging on his hand.

"I have to speak to Derek and see if he needs my help. If he doesn't, I'll come back and help with your fort."

They ran off and Ben turned to pick her up.

"I can walk."

"This is safer. You might hit a patch of ice," he said, silently calling himself a liar. He liked holding her in his arms too damned much. As soon as they stepped inside the kitchen, Derek turned from stirring a pot on the stove.

"Ahh, it's good to see you," he said, offering his hand to Ben and looking at Jennifer with curiosity.

"Jennifer, this is Derek Hansen, who runs the place. Derek, this is my stepsister, Jennifer Falcon."

"I think this place runs me," Derek replied easily, grinning and shaking hands with her.

"Pardon my appearance," Jennifer said, conscious of the torn and bloody slacks, "but I wrecked my car on the way here and this is all I have. Plus Ben's shirt."

Derek grinned. "You look great. We have enough jeans here to open a market. If you'd like, I can find you a clean pair."

"I'd love it, but I don't want to cause you trouble."

"It's done if I can put this guy to work first," he answered, looking at Ben.

"Sounds as if you need a hand," Ben observed.

"Martin is sick and can't cook, and the thermostat on the furnace isn't working."

Ben laughed. "One thing at a time. I don't know about cooking for your mob, but I can look at the thermostat."

"And I can cook," Jennifer said, shedding the parka and gloves.

"You don't have to work," Derek said.

"No, you don't. That wasn't why I brought you with me," Ben added.

"Go see about the thermostat," she replied, crossing the room to wash her hands.

Ben watched her and glanced at Derek and nodded. They left and he got his tools from the Jeep while Derek went to get jeans for Jennifer.

Thirty minutes later Ben had the thermostat in working order. He snapped shut the metal toolbox and headed for the kitchen. As he approached, he heard voices and laughter and he paused at the door. Wearing a white apron over faded trim jeans that hugged her hips and long legs, Jennifer was surrounded by five boys. She stood by the stove with Renzi standing on a chair beside her while he stirred something in a kettle. Dressed in an apron, Peter was beating eggs in a glass bowl.

"Careful now. Don't get too close to the stove," she cautioned.

"When can we lick the pan?" Johnny asked as he refilled the sugar canister. Timmy stood on a chair and rinsed dishes while Gregg watched Renzi stir.

"Is it my turn yet?" Gregg asked, looking at a timer clicking on the counter.

"Not quite," Jennifer said, resting a hand lightly on Renzi's shoulder as if she wanted to make certain he didn't get too close to the stove.

Remaining silent, his hip against the jamb, Ben watched them. Jennifer laughed when Renzi exclaimed over the big bubbles in the pot. She had all five boys organized and she was engrossed in them, turning first from one to another. The timer pinged. "Renzi, your turn is up," she said, taking the spoon from him and watching him climb down as Gregg climbed up.

"I want to stir," Peter said. "The nuts are ready."

Ben shifted and stepped back into the dining hall and went out another door so he wouldn't disturb them.

Several times during the day, he saw Jennifer as she worked with the boys. In spite of her foot, she helped serve lunch; in the afternoon she read to the preschool-age boys and sat at a table surrounded by boys that night.

Sixteen-year-old Todd sat beside her through dinner and afterward when she played a game with a dozen boys of various ages. It was obvious Todd was completely dazzled by Jennifer. Finally that night, Ben asked if Renzi could go home with them for a few days. "I'll bring him back by the end of the week," he told Derek.

"Sure. That's nice. She's great with the kids. I think Todd wants to ask her out."

Ben laughed. "She's a little old for him."

"I don't think he sees it that way."

When they finally piled into the Jeep, Todd stood at Jennifer's window and Derek stood talking to Ben while Renzi was buckled in the seat in the back.

Derek thrust his head close. "Jennifer, thanks a million for cooking. Martin should be able to cook tomorrow."

"Yeah, come back tomorrow," Todd said, waving and stepping back as Ben started the motor.

"You were a hit," Ben said when they drove away.

She flashed a smile. "Todd is incredibly young."

"He's sixteen, old lady. It couldn't have been too long ago you were that age yourself," Ben said, wondering about her because now she could recall her age.

"That was nine years ago, aeons ago when Mom married Weston. I'm twenty-four now, almost twenty-five."

"Can we play a game when we get to your house?" Renzi asked.

"Sure, we can," Ben answered easily. "I hope you know one," he said to Jennifer.

She shrugged and smiled again. In minutes she was leading them in songs, and as soon as they were settled at Ben's, she taught them a simple card game. Renzi sprawled on the floor in front of the fire, concentrating on cards spread before them while Jennifer sat curled up with her legs tucked under her. When the game was over, they drank cups of hot cocoa and Ben ran a bath for Renzi while Jennifer soaked her foot in warm water.

Jennifer found several of Ben's dog-eared children's books on his shelf and as soon as Renzi reappeared, she sat down to read to him. He sat beside her while Ben sat on the wing chair watching them, looking at Renzi twist the end of her braid in his small dark fingers. He had barely left her side most of the day and all evening and Ben felt another deep ache for him, wondering if he was so starved for mothering.

As she turned a page, Renzi tugged on the braid. "You're Ben's stepsister?"

"Yes."

"The stepsisters in books are mean."

"Well, I'm not mean," she said, smiling at him.

"If you're a stepsister, Ben can't marry you, can he?"

She swept a glance at Ben, meeting an amused gaze. "We're not blood relatives," Ben answered easily, watching her, "so we can marry, Renzi."

Renzi smiled as if the notion pleased him, and Ben grinned at her. Renzi looked at her again. "Would you marry Ben?"

She laughed. "I don't know Ben that well, Renzi. When people marry, it's special."

He thumped the book for her to go back to reading as if the whole notion had gone out of his head as swiftly as it had entered. Finally she looked up and closed the book. "He's asleep. Why don't you two take the bed tonight?"

Ben shook his head. "I already have a sleeping bag out and that's where he usually sleeps. He loves that down bag, and he'll be fine in here with me," Ben said as he stood to take Renzi from her arms. When he knelt down to slip his arms beneath the child, he looked into Jennifer's eyes. She was only inches away, watching Renzi, and then she seemed to realize Ben wasn't moving and she looked at him.

"You're good with him and the other boys. You must have worked with children before," Ben said softly.

She shook her head. "No. This is the first time I've ever really been around children for any length of time, but it was nice. I can see why you want to adopt him," she said, looking down at Renzi and smoothing locks of black hair from his face. "He loves you, too."

Ben wanted to lean forward and brush a kiss across her soft lips. All evening he had found himself forgetting why she was with him, forgetting Weston. She was warm, intelligent, companionable, fitting into his life like a missing piece of a puzzle. Curbing the impulse to kiss her, he picked up the child and carried him to the sleeping bag, kneeling to tuck him in.

Jennifer watched Ben, seeing the faded jeans mold his strong legs. He had taken her to the ranch today and brought Renzi home so she could see his relationship with the boys and why he didn't want to go to Dallas. She rubbed her forehead, because as much as Weston seemed to need Ben, Ben was important to the boys, too. But even if he went to Dallas, he could still adopt Renzi and take the child with him.

The next morning, sunshine was bright and hot and snow began to melt swiftly, dripping off sparkling icicles along the roof's edge. Ben stood at the kitchen window, sipping the last of his coffee, while Renzi and Jennifer finished breakfast. "Winter's over, I predict." He turned around. "Want to ride with me today?" he asked Renzi who glanced at Jennifer and then back to Ben. Renzi's eyes narrowed as if he were in deep thought.

"I'll stay here," he answered, and Ben bit back a laugh.

"Sure. I better get going." He grabbed his jacket off a peg and jammed the broad-brimmed Stetson on his head.

Jennifer followed Ben to the door. As Renzi left the kitchen and turned on the television in the next room, Ben's gaze shifted from Renzi to her.

"That's the first time he hasn't been hopping up and down to ride with me," Ben said with amusement, his dark eyes studying her.

"I'm a novelty. He's around men and horses all the time."

"Yeah," Ben answered softly. "I'd choose you over men and horses anytime."

She smiled, looking into his brown eyes, and she couldn't detect any of the anger that burned so steadily in him. He slid his finger beneath her chin and tilted her face up, leaning closer to her, making her pulse jump. She drew a deep breath, fires starting within her.

"Be careful, Jennifer," he drawled in a husky voice that played over her nerves like warm winds. "You walked into the wolf's lair to coax me back to Texas. You might find you like it here. Or you might find, when you go back, your feelings toward Weston have changed," Ben said solemnly in a deep voice.

Her reply was lost because he dipped his head, his mouth covering hers, his tongue an erotic invasion that seared every nerve. His arm went around her waist and she put her hands against his chest, feeling the soft suede of the coat, catching the clean scent of him. His tongue played over hers, repeating a rhythmic thrusting that was a heated hint of seduction.

He released her, his breathing as ragged as hers, his stormy gaze making her feel as if her insides were jelly. "I'll see you tonight," he said and left, a swish of cold air sweeping over her when he opened the door. He strode toward the barn, his long legs stretching out while his quiet words swirled in her mind. *You might find you like it here....*

She trembled, her body aching to have his arms around her and his mouth on hers again. She realized Ben was becoming important to her and it frightened her because not only did she want to avoid being caught between two men who had such opposing purposes, but she suspected Ben's heart hadn't been touched. He seemed a hard, tough man. And then she thought about Renzi and wondered if Ben was slowly softening.

Jennifer turned to clean the kitchen and then give attention to Renzi. She spent the day in activities with him, during the afternoon taking him for a short walk, Fella trotting beside them.

It was after dark when Jennifer heard the knob turn and Ben enter the kitchen. When he looked at her, she smiled, feeling her pulse catch. His jeans were mud spattered and he had a smear of dirt on his jaw, but he looked strong and virile and appealing. Renzi came running from the living area, rushing to Ben, who swung him up in a big hug.

"How's everybody here?"

"Okay," Renzi answered, his fingers touching Ben's jaw. "You're muddy." Laughing, Ben set him on his feet and shrugged out of his bulky coat. "Something smells good," he said while Renzi ran out of the room. He glanced at Jennifer who carried a plate to the table and stopped, catching his gaze going over her. She turned to face him, too conscious of the breadth of his shoulders, the intentness of his dark eyes.

"Ben, I talked to Weston today."

Six

Waiting, Ben gazed at her. "So what did he say?"

"I told him everything that had happened—"

"*Everything?*" Ben felt a flash of anger, remembering Madeline who calculated every provocative touch and kiss to help her get the bonus Weston had waiting if she brought Ben back to work at Falcon Enterprises. Ben edged closer, placing his hand against Jennifer's cheek. "Did you tell him how much I like to kiss you?" he asked in a low voice, aware of Renzi in the next room watching television.

Fires flared in her eyes, and she jerked her head away from him, raising her chin. "You listen to me, Ben Falcon," she said, her cheeks turning pink while she jabbed his chest with her forefinger. "I'm not plotting every move with him. I came up here to talk and appeal to you to go home to the father who needs you. It's ludicrous to think I intend to bargain for that with my body!"

He gave a snarl in his throat, refuting her words, and she stiffened with fury. Waving her hand, she glowered at him.

"What have you got to give up? A ranch you're just start-ing? You can have a ranch in Texas and keep this one on what he would pay you. You said you might want to adopt Renzi," she added in a whisper, glancing toward the living area. "You can take him to Dallas as easily as you can keep him here, and he'd get a better education in a city, and you'd be better able to provide for him."

"Not necessarily, but that's beside the point. Calm down, woman. What *did* you tell Weston?"

"I told him about my wreck and the temporary amnesia. Because of your message he had discussed my amnesia with doctors in Dallas. Of course he knew about the storms. He said to take whatever time I need, but he wants you back badly. His blood pressure is up again and he's been having some mild chest pains."

"Well, I agree with Weston on one thing—you can sure as hell take all the time you want," Ben drawled. "I'll go to town tomorrow and you can go along and I'll get you some clothes. You're going to be a guest for a hell of a long time if you wait until I go back with you."

"No, I won't. I'll go back to Dallas soon whether you go with me or not. I need to get back to my job," she replied solemnly, her gaze going over his features. "And any time you want me out of your house, say so. Weston's sending me money, so now I can repay you and get another plane ticket to go home."

Ben nodded and turned away. "I'll clean up for dinner," he said, crossing the room, feeling a strange sense of loss with her words about a ticket home. He sat down to pull off his muddy boots, placing them by the door. "Spring is here and the snow is thawing." He glanced up at her. "I saw the snow bunny you and Renzi built today."

"There's still plenty of snow. Renzi had a good time."

Ben headed for the bedroom, thinking how right it seemed to have her in his house. But she came with strings that were attached straight back to Weston and Dallas.

Shackles was more like it, and he wanted no part of them, but damn, she was nice to have around and nice to kiss. He stripped off the muddy clothes and showered, washing his hair and drying it, pulling on jeans and a plaid woolen shirt.

Supper was a roast with fluffy mashed potatoes, steamed carrots and a green salad. When they were finished eating, Renzi and Jennifer cleared the table and Ben loaded the dishwasher. Finally they settled in front of the fire for more card games and stories.

During the night a storm blew in, a loud clap of thunder rattling panes and waking Ben. Remembering Renzi's fear of thunderstorms, Ben sat up quickly and swung his feet to the floor. The sleeping bag was empty. Another loud clap of thunder banged as he yanked on his jeans. Fella was gone, as well. Ben turned toward his bedroom where the door was ajar. As he reached the door, he heard Jennifer's soft voice.

"...and Mr. Thunder said, 'The sky is mine!' and he boomed and boomed. Mr. Lightning crackled and popped and streaked across the sky. He said, 'The sky is not yours! It's mine and I'll keep it, and you can't have it. You're not important. You're only loud noise. I'm full of fire and power and I can light up the earth and burn where I strike.'"

Lightning flashed, illuminating the room. Jennifer was on her side, her arm around Renzi who had scooted close to her under the covers. Fella lay on the floor beside the bed and thumped his tail as he looked at Ben. The flash was gone instantly, but another clap of thunder came and Fella whimpered and Renzi called to him.

"Here, Fella. He's scared, too."

Fella jumped onto the bed and Ben moved into the room as lightning flashed again.

"Renzi, I don't want Fella on my bed. Down, Fella," he ordered. "Renzi, do you want to come back in here, so Jennifer can get to sleep?"

"No, sir. You can get in bed with us."

Amusement came as lightning flashed, and he met Jennifer's wide-eyed solemn gaze. "No, I can't."

"Why not? There's room for you. Jennifer's telling a story about thunder and lightning."

"You go ahead with your story," he said quietly, looking at her in the darkness. "Want me to take Renzi?"

"No, of course not," she answered quietly. "We're fine. I don't even mind Fella."

"I don't want him to get accustomed to sleeping on my bed."

"He doesn't hurt anything," Renzi said.

"He sheds hair and his paws are probably dirty." Ben threw up his hand. "Oh, heck, let him stay." He left the room and heard Renzi's high voice.

"Finish telling me about Mr. Lightning and Mr. Thunder." Before Jennifer could speak, another boom of thunder vibrated through the house. "I'm scared."

"It's all right, Renzi."

"Are you scared?"

"No, not of thunder and lightning. Thunder is just noisy."

"Are you ever scared of anything?"

Ben knew he should walk away, but he stood immobile, wondering what she would tell Renzi, listening to her calm voice as she talked to the child.

"I'm scared of things, scared if people I love are all right when I'm away from them."

"Who do you love?"

"I love my stepfather."

"Do you love me?"

"Yes, Renzi, I love you," she reassured him so quietly that Ben barely heard the words, and he hurt again because of the longing that was plain in Renzi's voice. If his mother didn't want him, Ben was definitely going ahead with the adoption proceedings. Maybe if he made mistakes in parenting, the love he had for Renzi would make up for them.

"I love you, too," Renzi answered with the total giving of a young child. "Do you love Ben?"

"I don't know Ben that well."

"You know him as well as you know me."

"Do you want to hear about Mr. Lightning?"

Ben moved away from the door on bare feet. The floor was cold, but he barely noticed, thinking about Jennifer in his big bed. She was so good with Renzi and the boys. He moved to the fire to place logs on it and light them, knowing that he wouldn't sleep. He moved to the window and watched rain stream down. Snow and now rain. The streams would be swollen, the rivers up and running. How long would she stay? And how empty would the house be when she left? Every day he was finding it more difficult to keep from touching her. Each kiss stirred him more.

Today when he was working, he had stepped into a hole and sunk in mud to his knees because he was lost in thought about her, remembering their kiss this morning before he left the house.

Lightning flashed and showed silvery rivulets of water streaming across the ground. As soon as warm weather came, with all this water, the earth would green up fast. Ben rubbed the back of his neck. How bad was Weston? He couldn't imagine Weston incapacitated. Or even cutting back. And why did Weston want him back when he had Jordan? Jordan had always cozied up to Weston, always made it clear that Falcon Enterprises was the most important thing in his life. Jordan always seemed to please him, so why send Jennifer up here?

Ben had no answers, thinking about Jennifer's view of his father as a man who had taken her out of poverty and been so good to her. Had marriage to Jennifer's mother mellowed Weston? It was difficult for Ben to imagine, but was he being fair to Jennifer in dismissing everything she said? He thought of the times Weston had tried to bribe him or

coerce him into going back. He remembered the women and
their lies. If Jennifer was telling the truth, should he at least
listen?

Warm weather came and the earth began to blossom while
Renzi spent the rest of the week with them, going to town
where Ben bought him a new pair of boots, jeans, a shirt
and a jacket. Jennifer bought new clothes, as well. Ben
glimpsed her when she walked out of a shop and crossed the
street to meet them. His pulse drummed as his gaze went
over her new jeans that clung to her hips, the cotton blouse
that couldn't hide the slight bounce of her full breasts as she
hurried toward them, and the sexy sway of her hips now that
she could walk without difficulty. He was going to miss her
when she went back to Texas, and the notion surprised him.

On Sunday they took Renzi back to the ranch and spent
the day while Ben did minor repairs and Jennifer stayed with
the boys. When she kissed Renzi goodbye, he clung to her
neck and she picked him up. They stood beside Ben's Jeep
with stars shining brightly overhead while Todd and Derek
talked to Ben.

"Will you come back?" Renzi asked her.

"I don't know, Renzi," she answered truthfully, hurting
because he was a loving child and she couldn't bear to think
she would inflict even the tiniest ache because of parting. "I
have to go home to Texas soon."

"You'll come back and see Ben, won't you?" he asked.

"I don't know. I'll write to you and I'll call you on the
phone." She kissed his cheek and set him down. He held her
tightly, pulling her down and kissing her cheek.

"I love you," he said quietly. "Please come back and see
me."

She hugged him and stood to find Ben watching her while
he talked to Derek.

Todd moved closer and held out his hand. "I hope you
come back, Jennifer."

"Thanks, Todd," she replied, shaking hands with him.

"You guys get back and let the lady get into the Jeep," Derek said good-naturedly and opened the door for her while Ben hugged Renzi.

"Bye, guy. See you next weekend. So long, Todd, Derek," Ben said and slid behind the wheel, slamming the door closed while the three stepped back from Jennifer's door. Ben started the motor and headed home.

"A few more times there and Todd will follow us home to be with you."

"Mmm," came a muffled answer. Ben glanced at Jennifer and felt a shock because she was pinching the bridge of her nose and he realized she was either crying or struggling to avoid doing so. He slowed and stopped, putting the Jeep in Park and turning her to face him. Tears brimmed in her eyes and she raised her chin and wiped at the tears.

"Now maybe you understand why I can't leave here."

"That doesn't have anything to do with it being hard to tell Renzi goodbye," she said, looking at her fingers entwined in her lap, her head bent and her words muffled.

"The hell it doesn't," he snapped, annoyed that she clung so stubbornly to getting him to Texas when she could see what held him here and she felt some love for the homeless boys, too. He threw the Jeep in gear and drove in silence, trying to avoid big puddles in the road, his anger rising.

"If you adopted Renzi, he would be better off in Dallas."

"Not necessarily. Kids out here get good educations and they grow up loving the land and knowing how to live on it. Where did you grow up?"

"All over oil country. Louisiana, Oklahoma, Texas, California."

They rode in silence and when they reached the house, he let her out at the back door. "I'll put the Jeep away."

"I'll ride with you," she replied, surprising him, and he drove to the garage.

They climbed out and started walking back, their feet on the gravel drive the only sound in the night. He glanced at her to find her looking at the stars and he turned her to face him. "You know Renzi would have a good life living out here. Besides, his mother may take him back, so it's pointless to argue about what ifs."

Jennifer lowered her head and wiped her eyes again and he frowned, realizing she was really torn up over the child. He placed his hand on her shoulder and tilted her face up. "You're going back to Texas and you barely know the kid—"

"I've never been around a little kid or even thought about having one and he seemed so vulnerable. He hugged me and told me he loved me and he wants me to come back to see him and I can't."

Against all good judgment, Ben pulled her close, wrapping his arms around her.

"I hope you adopt him. I hope someone loves him and cares for him."

"He gets good care where he is," Ben replied solemnly. "And he knows I love him."

"Do you tell him, Ben?" she asked, leaning back to look up at him. "You're so tough and hard—do you ever tell him?"

Moonlight shone on her. Her full lips were only inches away and a tempting invitation. "I tell him," he answered, fighting the impulse to kiss her. "And I do what I can to show him. He knows I love him." His thoughts had shifted from Renzi to her. Ben tightened his arms and bent his head to kiss her.

Her mouth opened beneath his and she returned his kiss. His heart thudded as her hips thrust against him. He longed to touch and kiss and discover her, to bury himself in her warmth, and he fought an inner battle with himself, wanting this woman who was beginning to fill voids in his life.

When she pulled away, both were breathing hard. They stared at each other, desire burning in him while the argument between them created an insurmountable obstacle. She turned, and they walked to the house in silence.

Inside, she disappeared into the bedroom, closing the door behind her while Fella trailed after Ben. Ben's thoughts were stormy, still cursing Weston, silently berating Jennifer for being so blind and stubborn. She loved Renzi a great deal to cry over him like that, so how could she still ask him to leave this place?

Ben built a fire and removed his boots and thought about how silent the house was and knew it would be that way again when she went home. And maybe after tonight, she would go. Maybe she was in her room packing to go now. The thought made his insides knot because he liked having her around in spite of the differences between them. He moved restlessly, staring at the closed door.

An hour later as he sat with the paper in his hands, staring at words and yet not reading them, her door opened and she came out.

She crossed the room to sit on the sofa. "I have to go home soon. This is getting us nowhere and it's too difficult on both of us. Please, tonight, think about going with me."

"Have you been talking to Weston?" She raised her chin and looked him in the eye and he knew the answer before she replied.

"Yes, I have. I called him a little while ago."

"Did you tell him you're coming home?"

"No, I haven't, because I wanted to ask you one more time to give some thought to your answer."

"I have been."

They gazed at each other and he could feel the tension crackle between them. The phone rang, breaking the spell, and he crossed the room to answer it. He turned to Jennifer, amusement easing the stiffness in his shoulders as he carried the phone to her. "Todd wants to talk to you."

Going to the kitchen, Ben could hear her cheerful tone as she talked to Todd. He got a glass of water and drank it down, moving around the kitchen and getting things ready for early morning. He finally returned to sit in front of the fire, glancing at Jennifer who laughed.

"I'll think about it, Todd. If I'm still at Ben's, I'll see you again. Tell Derek thank-you for the offer." After a pause, she spoke again, "I better go now. Thanks, Todd. Sure." Another pause and then she gave a Dallas number. "Okay, good night, Todd." She replaced the receiver and glanced at Ben. "Maybe I better go home soon. They said they wanted me to come with you next Sunday. They'll bake a cake if I will."

Ben grinned at her. "Todd would go to Texas with you in a minute."

"Are all of them so starved for love?" she asked, setting the phone on a table.

"Todd isn't doing this because he's starved for love," Ben remarked dryly. "Not the kind you're talking about. He's suffering sixteen-year-old lust."

"That's ridiculous."

"No, it's not. You're young and beautiful."

"Not that young, thank you."

He chuckled and she smiled in return, and while he told himself he was being a fool, he stood and moved to the sofa beside her. She was curled in the corner with her feet tucked under her. He placed one arm on the back of the sofa, one on the sofa arm, hemming her in with his body as he studied her, thinking he had never seen such crystal-green eyes in his life.

"Todd's got damned good taste."

She inhaled, the deep breath thrusting her breasts at him more noticeably. He glanced down and then looked up at her again while an inner voice told him he was asking for trouble.

"Who's the guy in your life?"

"There isn't one."

"I thought I ought to ask," he said.

"Ben," she said, pushing against his chest, something flickering in the depths of her eyes when she touched him. He knew that instant response was one thing about her that turned him on. "Let's not complicate things any more than they already are," she said. Her wide-eyed gaze locked with his, her face only inches from him. He could catch some kind of sweet scent from her.

"Sure." He slid his arm around her waist and leaned forward to kiss her, and in minutes she was on his lap, cradled in his arms as he leaned over her and kissed her, his hand beneath her shirt, cupping her breast. Suddenly she pushed his hand away and stood, shaking her head at him.

"No. I will not be caught between you and Weston. You're a tough man, Ben, and I won't go home hurt. I don't know whether you're doing that because you want me or because you want to get back at Weston—"

"Dammit!"

She turned and went into his bedroom and closed the door behind her. Clenching his fists, he let her go while he ached and wanted her. It was Weston's stepdaughter he desired! He knew he should leave the woman alone and let her get the hell back to Texas.

Ben moved across the room, anger rising as he glared at the closed door. She had charged into his life, causing him trouble from the first flash of orange when her car had gone off the mountain. He placed his hands on his hips and stared at her door and made a decision about the next day.

When she came in for breakfast, he turned to her, his gaze drifting over her blue cotton blouse and jeans that emphasized her narrow waist and long legs. "Before you go back, I have something I want to show you. Can you ride a horse?"

"Yes."

"I want you to go with me this morning."

For a moment he thought she would refuse him, but then she nodded her head.

"Good," he remarked, and glanced at the window where the sky was still dark. "The weather should be clear."

They ate in silence, and half an hour later they rode away from the barn. He had pulled a jean jacket over his chambray shirt and had given Jennifer a jacket.

Jennifer inhaled, catching the strong aroma of spruce and a faint smell of leather from the saddles. The sun was still below the treetops, mist clinging on low-lying land like fallen clouds. Birdcalls were melodic and the steady clop of the horses was a peaceful sound. As Ben rode ahead, she looked at his hat sitting squarely on his head, his broad shoulders that looked larger in a jean jacket and she wondered about him. What would it have been like if they could have known each other without Weston and Falcon Enterprises between them?

They rode all morning, Ben leaving her once when he spotted some stray steers. After he rounded them up, she rode with him to drive them back to the herd. She watched him work, riding his horse with ease, handling the animals competently.

Midday, they took a narrow trail up a mountain. It was cool and dark beneath the branches of tall pines. They came out of the trees onto a sunny stretch of open land near the top of the mountain. Wind whistled through the pines and her breath caught at the sight spread before her. Ben dismounted and she did the same, looking at the panorama below. In the distance she could glimpse the rooftops of his house and outbuildings. Snow-capped mountains rose against the blue blanket of sky, and far below she could see the sparkling creek winding along the valley floor. She turned to find Ben watching her. He had shed his hat and jacket and stood with his hands on his jean-clad hips.

Sunshine was warm on her shoulders and she removed her jacket, dropping it down on the ground. Wind caught her hair and tugged short tendrils out of the clip fastened behind her head.

She rolled back her sleeves slightly as she studied him. "You brought me with you today for the same reason you took me to the boys' ranch and you brought Renzi home."

"No. I bring Renzi home with me often."

"All right. You brought me with you so I'd see what a beautiful place you have here."

"Yes. I'm not leaving it. I've found peace here that I never had in Texas."

"Does it matter to you that Weston really needs you now?"

"He thinks he needs me. He has Jordan."

"Jordan can't do what you'd do, and Weston knows that. He's told me so."

Ben felt his anger rise just thinking about Weston's arguments. He remembered the abuse and the cruelty.

She moved closer to Ben. "You don't have to give this up. Get someone to run it while you come back for a few years."

"A few years! Weston has had so many years of my life already! He had the first seventeen. He had the years I worked for him."

She placed her hand on his arm. "Ben, please," she asked, her voice softening, and suddenly he remembered Madeline and her seduction and how it had all been for Weston. He still wasn't certain whether Jennifer was leading up to the same thing for the same reason.

"You go back to Texas, Jennifer, and tell Weston that the answer is no," Ben said, grinding out the words.

Seven

——

Jennifer inhaled swiftly and then she spun on her heel and headed toward the horses. Ben watched her go and suddenly he had to hold her one more time, kiss her once more before she walked out of his life. In long strides Ben caught her, turning her.

He hauled her into his arms, his mouth stopping her protest. He bent over her, his tongue going deep into her soft mouth, tasting her, muffling her moan. For an instant she resisted, stiffening as if she would push him away. And then she quivered and responded, her tongue entering his mouth as if neither could fight the attraction they felt at every level.

He knew he should stop and avoid complications in his life, but he wanted her softness, her warmth. He stepped closer, spreading his legs apart, pulling her close against him, cupping her round bottom to pull her up against him.

His fingers found the clasp to the barrette and he pulled it loose, tossing it aside and letting her hair swing free. He ran his hand through the silky mass while he kissed her, and his arousal was swift, throbbing, urgent.

With every kiss, Jennifer knew she was binding herself more strongly to a man who would never leave his mountain home. She wanted to turn and walk away from him, but when he had touched her, she melted instantly into his arms, unable to resist, astounded that this handsome, virile man would shake because of her kisses, that he wanted her with a heat that might consume them both.

His fingers twisted the buttons of her shirt, fumbling and trembling until he pushed away the cotton and unclasped her lacy pink bra. His hand cupped her breast, his thumb circling her nipple, and she gasped with pleasure.

Ben leaned back to look at her, his pulse pounding and roaring in his ears. Her eyes were closed, her head thrown back as she gripped his shoulders. Her breasts were full, pink tipped, the nipples hardened peaks. He cupped both breasts, her softness making him feel as if he would explode with need, and all his reason and caution flew like the wind over the mountain.

He wanted this woman as he had never wanted any other. He wanted her soft warmth, her fiery response, her fullness for living. And he had wanted her since the first hours he had brought her home from the wreck. His fingers slipped down to her jeans and as he unbuttoned them, he leaned forward to kiss her again.

She trembled beneath his touch, kissing him wildly, one arm wrapped around his neck, her other hand drifting over him, sliding down to his waist and over his hip and along his thigh like liquid fire pouring over him. His nerves were raw, longing tearing at him while he pushed away her jeans and slid his hands to her hips.

Lost in his kisses and caresses, Jennifer knew she should stop him, yet everything in her wanted his loving. She wanted his strong arms around her, his hands seeking her. She wanted his strength and vigor, wanted to know that he found her desirable. She wanted to be a woman, complete, loved, and she wanted it to be with Ben because she had never responded to any man the way she did to him. She had been unresponsive with other men, she realized now, as if she had been waiting all her life for this man and his touch.

She ran her fingers in his thick hair, feeling the coolness on her skin when he slid down her jeans. He knelt to pull off her loafers and he glanced up at her. Her hands were on his shoulders as he removed her shoes and pulled away her jeans. His gaze drifted over her languidly. "You're beautiful," he said roughly, and her pulse raced beneath his look. He stood, his hands sliding up over her thighs, her waist and ribs, up to her breasts as he bent his head to take her nipple in his mouth, his tongue hot and wet against her flesh. She closed her eyes, swaying toward him while his strong arm went around her waist.

She felt him move away for a moment and he yanked off his shirt. Jennifer inhaled, running her hands across his chest, over his taut flesh and powerful muscles. His hand slipped along her thigh, making her moan softly as he kissed her. She knew she had passed the moment to stop, that she had made a commitment. She opened her eyes, glancing up at him as he watched her, his midnight eyes filled with so much blatant desire that his look was as arousing to her as his caresses. Never had she wanted a man like she did him. She drew a deep breath, the realization sweeping through her and shaking her more than his touch had—she was in love with him.

She closed her eyes, trying to shut out the thought, because all it could mean was heartbreak. But right now she was going to take what he offered and love him in return even if tomorrow they parted forever. All her life she had lived with caution and consequences and this one moment she was following her heart.

"Jenny," he whispered, kissing her ear, trailing kisses to her mouth, his mouth covering hers as he kissed her hard.

One arm banded her waist, and Ben pulled her close against him, turning slightly so he could caress her legs. He slipped his hand between her thighs, feeling the tremor run through her and then his hand caressed her soft folds, his palm starting the intimate friction that could drive her to the brink. While he kissed her, she clung to him, her fingers digging into his shoulders and when she was wrapped in passion, he raised his head to look at her. Her hips writhed against him, her white teeth were biting into her lower lip, her eyes tightly closed. Her body glistened now with a sheen of sweat. She was alabaster and pink, temptation and warmth.

She grasped his arms, her eyes flying open. "Ben," she whispered, "please—"

With his pulse roaring, he unfastened his belt and jeans to free his erect member, shoving down his jeans, not taking time to remove them or his boots.

Ben pulled Jennifer down on his shirt, rolling over on top of her and spreading her legs. She watched him and his heart pounded and somewhere in dim recesses was a voice that said, *Fool, fool...*

He covered her mouth, kissing her deeply, feeling her arms go around him. She held him and raised her hips to meet him and Ben touched her with his manhood and then slipped inside her partially and felt the obstruction.

Shock jolted him and his eyes flew wide as he looked at her. She caught his buttocks, her hands firm against him as she wrapped her long legs around him. "Oh, Ben," she whispered, looking up at him.

"Jenny, you're a virgin!"

She shifted, raising her hips, her green eyes watching him. "Ben..." she whispered, her legs holding him tightly.

He leaned back. "Jenny, you're not protected—"

He started to move away and she gave a cry, holding him. "Ben, please..." Her green eyes were fiery, burning with desire.

Making a decision, he watched her as he yanked his bill-fold from the hip pocket of his jeans and reached for the small packet so she would be protected. Her gaze never wavered, her hands drifting over him while he put the condom in place, her fingertips igniting fires along his thighs until he knew he would lose control. His thoughts were a turmoil and every grain of sense told him to stop, but one look into her green eyes and he couldn't.

His stormy thoughts vanished as her hands slid over his hips. Coming down over her, he covered her mouth and eased into her softness, feeling the obstruction, partially withdrawing and entering slowly again, driving her to urgency and then finally thrusting deep.

Jennifer's cry was muffled as she moved beneath him, hurting, yet wanting him desperately at this moment, wanting his strength and love, wanting his long hard body and so much more of him, knowing this would be the most she would get.

And then thought vanished as he began to move faster. Pain blurred and need rippled through her, an urgency that made her move with him, her body shuddering as he took her to a brink. Her pulse drowned out all sounds and blinding light seemed to explode behind her closed eyes as she was enveloped in sensation, a rapturous burst of release. She barely heard his hoarse cry of her name while she longed for a cry of love from him.

"Ben, my love," she whispered, unable to hold back the words yet hoping he didn't hear her.

She felt his shuddering release, his body reacting as he turned his head to kiss her savagely, a hunger in his kiss that seemed to burn to her soul and make her wonder what he really did feel.

His arms tightened around her and he held her while their breathing returned to normal. He brushed her hair away from her face and trailed kisses from her temple to her mouth, raising and bracing himself on his elbows to look down at her.

Jennifer could see the questions in his eyes and knew he was worrying about her. She pulled his head down to kiss him slowly, deliberately and in seconds he returned her kiss until he pulled away to look at her again.

He rolled onto his side, turning her with him, their legs tangled as he wrapped her in his arms and gazed at her solemnly. "You've never gone with anyone."

"I did when I was in college. He was older and was back in college to get a doctorate." Her voice lowered, and her gaze slid down as her fingers played on his chest. "I'm old-fashioned. In my mother's life, before Weston, there was a steady stream of men. I think she did it to get back at Billy because I'm sure he wasn't faithful to her. I didn't want that. I wanted to be so very sure."

Ben watched her, seeing the slight frown, silently calling himself all kinds of names for what he had just done and knowing he couldn't give her the commitment she must want and had waited so long to find. Instead, she had given herself to him knowing there wouldn't be one.

A pink flush crept up her cheeks, and he leaned closer to hear her. "I found out Devin was seeing someone else. I think he dated me because of Weston's money. When I confronted him about the other woman, he said I was frigid, incapable of passion—"

Ben swore and turned her to look at him. "That's a damn lie," he said quietly.

"He wasn't the first or the last man to tell me that."

"Then they just wanted sex with you and when you wouldn't, the accusations were a way to soothe their egos."

Her arm tightened around his neck and she looked into his eyes, her cheeks becoming pinker. "Ben, I wanted you to love me. I know there's no commitment and can't be because of the disagreement between us." She moved so her face was buried against his neck and he suspected she was trying to ease his conscience. "I wanted you."

"Oh, Jenny," he said, tightening his arms around her and shifting to turn her face up to kiss her, feeling as if she had given him so much more than her body and knowing he couldn't give back to her all she wanted. The kiss lengthened and then his hand slid over her body, following her curves. He leaned back and moved away, standing and holding out his hand to help her up. "Let's go back to the house and do this right."

Her green eyes darkened and her gaze swept over him. He was aroused again, his shaft erect and ready. Blushing, she stood naked before him, but with desire in her eyes, and he wanted her more than he had earlier. She turned to gather up her clothes and he pulled his on, unable to take his gaze from her. The cut on her thigh was healing and none of the cuts or fading bruises detracted from her beauty. He felt dazzled by her, angered at himself, and yet he wanted her again.

When they were dressed, he helped her onto the saddle and then he mounted his horse and they wound down the mountain, Jennifer trailing behind him.

She studied him, her pulse pounding because she knew they were going home and he would make love to her again. She had seen how aroused he was as he dressed, still amazed at the reaction he had to her. She had called the airlines early this morning, and late tomorrow afternoon she was taking a flight from Albuquerque to Dallas. As she rode behind Ben, she wondered whether she would ever see him or Renzi again.

At the barn she waited while Ben unsaddled the horses and watered and fed them. Draping his arm across her shoulders and carrying their jackets, he walked beside her to the house.

Inside, he tossed the coats on a kitchen chair and led her to the bedroom where he turned her to face him. As soon as she looked up into his dark eyes, she felt her body respond as heat suffused her and her breasts tightened. His hands went to the buttons of her blue cotton blouse.

"Let's take a shower," he said in a husky voice that played over her nerves.

She slid her hands across his shoulders and knew she should tell him about the plane reservation. Her hands drifted down to his belt and he inhaled swiftly as she tugged at the brass buckle. She glanced up at him. "I can't believe I can arouse you like this."

"Oh, Jenny, you can!" He bent his head, his mouth covering hers as he kissed her, his tongue sliding with a tantalizing slowness over her lower lip, touching the insides of her mouth, hot and wet strokes over her tongue that made her shake. She twisted loose the buttons on his jeans, feeling his hard maleness.

He moved away to sit down and tug off his boots and she continued to undress beneath his gaze, his dark eyes like caresses to her flesh as she pulled off the blouse and dropped it to the floor and pushed down her jeans to step out of them.

"I'll have to unwrap my foot to shower."

"I'll do that," he said. He stood and stepped out of his jeans and briefs and crossed the room to her to pick her up in his arms. His flesh was heated, and she was conscious of every place they touched each other as he held her and kissed her.

"To hell with the shower," he whispered, placing his knee on the bed and moving between her legs to kiss the inside of her thigh.

"Ben, your spread—" The notion was gone as his tongue slid along her thigh. She arched beneath him, raising up slightly to watch him, tangling her fingers in his hair. Suddenly she pushed him up, so that he was on his knees and she could reach his engorged shaft. She curled her fingers around him and he groaned, his hand winding in her hair.

She flicked out her tongue, stroking him, touching the thick velvet tip, feeling his fingers dig into her shoulder. "I'm so sure of what I want," she whispered, knowing he had driven away some of the demons that had haunted her since Devin.

He pulled her up, his eyes burning with desire as he hauled her into his embrace to kiss her hungrily. They went down on the bed and he entered her slowly. She arched to meet him as he tried to maintain control and give her more pleasure this time.

While her pulse roared, Jennifer clung to him as he filled her, so hot and hard. He withdrew and eased into her again and again until she was wild with wanting him and held his firm buttocks, her legs tightly wrapped around him. "Ben, please . . ."

He thrust deeply, taking her into awareness only of sensation. They moved together and then his control was gone and he drove fast and hard, hearing her cry dimly over his own thundering heart.

"Jenny . . ." He turned to kiss her, wanting to be united with her as much as humanly possible, feeling as if she had brought warmth and love after years of solitude and loneliness. His lean body moved with hers until he felt her shudder. "Oh, Jennifer," he whispered, then exploded his own release.

She held her breath, waiting for words that might follow. Instead, he turned his head to kiss her and she told herself she was foolish to expect declarations of love.

Ben wrapped her in his arms and rolled to his side, holding her close and stroking her. He kissed her long and hard while she placed her fingers against his cheek, drawing them down over his jaw.

Jennifer was lost in wonderment, marveling over his body, relishing being held, wanting to look at him and touch him. She drew her finger along a faint scar across his shoulder. "What's this from?"

"A rodeo. Bull riding."

"Your life is so different from mine," she said, looking up at him, wanting the moment never to end and knowing it had to. And knowing what she had to tell him.

"Ben, I've made reservations. I'm going home tomorrow."

Eight

—

Feeling a sense of loss, Ben looked down at her. He stroked damp locks of hair away from her temples. "Change your reservations. Wait a few days, hon."

Startled green eyes looked up at him as he slid his hand over her smooth back. She pulled away from him and sat up. "If I wait a few days," she said solemnly, "I'll never want to go. I have to leave tomorrow." And all the time she spoke, she kept hearing his casual endearment, *hon*. He meant little by it, yet it warmed her as much as his touch.

Ben studied her and wanted to argue and talk her into staying, and he thought he could, yet he knew it wouldn't be fair to her. He wasn't going to make a commitment to a woman whose life and love and career were tied up with Weston. Ben clamped his jaw closed and rolled off the bed, leaning over to pick her up. "Let's have that shower," he said in a husky voice, shoving thoughts of tomorrow out of mind.

She wound her arm around his neck as she gazed at him. "Do you think that's wise?"

"I think it's the smartest suggestion I've made in months," he answered with a wide grin that made her heart miss beats.

He hadn't argued with her about staying, but had accepted her answer, and she felt the kernel of hurt that she knew was going to grow into a dreadful heartache. She shoved it aside, not wanting anything to cloud the present moment with him. Ben made her feel fully a woman, desirable and sexy, a heady feeling she had never experienced. He turned on the water, then sat her down on a bench in the large bathroom and knelt to unwrap the Ace bandage from her foot. When he finished, he stood and leaned over her, sliding his hand behind her head.

"Let me show you how we'll do this so you won't have to put any weight on your foot."

"I can manage. I've been walking without difficulty."

"My way is much better." He kissed her, silencing her argument as his tongue met hers. Needs that had seemed so satisfied only moments earlier now rekindled.

He picked her up in his arms so she straddled him and he carried her to the shower while he kissed her, but she was barely aware of anything except his strong arms and body, his mouth on hers. Warm water hit her, splashing over them, but she was only dimly aware of it as the tip of his erection touched her in exquisite torment.

"Ben!"

He lowered her, his shaft sliding into her and she closed her eyes, moving against him while he took her again to rapture.

By nightfall, sprawled in his big bed, she stirred drowsily, feeling his arm tighten around her. "Ben, this is decadent. Suppose someone needs you and calls or comes to the house."

"They can go away," he drawled, turning on his side to look at her, combing his fingers through her long hair and making her scalp tingle. She was so beautiful, so warm, so damned desirable. And so involved with Weston.

"Want some dinner?" he asked.

"Now that you mention it, the idea of food is appealing."

Ben rolled on top of her, feeling her softness, her full breasts pressed against him. "I'll tell you what sounds appealing—"

"Ben Falcon, you promised food!"

"In a minute," he said softly, amazed how swiftly she could arouse him. "I'm too old for this," he muttered, trailing kisses from her ear to the corner of her mouth. "You're doing it again," he whispered as his erection thrust against her thigh.

"*I'm* doing it! It seems to me as if you're—"

He kissed her and the dance began again, and dimly in the recesses of his mind was astonishment that each time his need for her seemed to grow instead of diminish. What would his life be like tomorrow after she had gone?

Later as they lay quietly—Jennifer wrapped in his arms and her leg thrown across his—he stared at the ceiling and thought about Texas. Under no circumstances would he go back to work for Weston. Weston had driven all love and loyalty out of him years ago and his heart was with Renzi and the boys and his ranch. But Ben faced the fact that he could go see Weston and maybe bury some of the sharpest animosity that had burned between them. Ben had to laugh at himself over that one. *You're still at it, buddy. The eternal hope that a father will have some shred of love for you.* Weston loved money and power and damned little else.

Ben thought about the ranch and the things he would have to juggle and change if he were to fly out of here tomorrow with Jennifer. He kissed her temple, then eased himself away from her and stood, pulling on his jeans. When he turned around and glanced at her, he felt his heart clench. Her auburn hair was spread over the pillow and a sheet was across her, leaving her shoulders and slender arms and one leg bare. She looked tempting and beautiful and as if she belonged there. For just a moment he remembered the night he had stepped into the bedroom and found Renzi with her. If only she had no ties to Dallas—

He clamped his jaw closed tightly and turned for the kitchen, trying to avoid banging pans as he got a package of trout he had caught and cleaned and frozen. Setting the fish under a stream of cold water to thaw, he put rice on to cook.

Thirty minutes later, he heard a noise behind him and turned to find Jennifer standing in the doorway. She wore one of his shirts and leaned against the jamb. Her hair was damp from washing and her face scrubbed and he forgot about food.

"You can cook, too," she said in a sexy drawl that made him grin and wipe his hands and cross the room to put his arms around her.

"The minute you stepped through the door, I lost all interest in cooking," he said.

"Did you now?" she asked in a teasing voice and he made a sound deep in his throat like a growl as he tightened his arms to pull her against him.

"With talk like that, you'll never get your dinner," he said, bending down to kiss her.

Time and thought spun away as she clung to him and returned his kisses and didn't care whether she ate tonight or not. Dimly she thought she smelled something, but it was in the recesses of thought. Suddenly a strident alarm went off and she pulled away.

"Ben!"

"Dammit!" The kitchen was filled with smoke curling along the ceiling, setting off a smoke alarm. He yanked a burning pan off a burner and set it in the sink, turning on water and sending up a cloud of steam while he ran to the door to yank it open. He pulled out a chair, stepped up on it and disengaged the smoke alarm. Quiet returned. He looked down at her from the chair.

"Don't you dare laugh," he said, dropping to the floor. Smoke stung her eyes and she felt amazement that her kisses had driven everything from his mind. He fanned the smoke as cool air filled the room.

"Where's Fella?"

"He must have decided he'd have a better time at the bunkhouse," Ben said dryly as he closed the door. He crossed the room to her and her pulse jumped. She held her hand out against his chest.

"Maybe we better see about the rest of dinner."

He studied her and nodded, turning away. "I'll put the fish on the grill. I was waiting until you got up. I was cooking rice and that's what burned."

"I won't cry over rice," she answered, watching him pour two glasses of wine and bring one to her. Their fingers brushed as she took the glass from him and gazed into his dark eyes that had sinfully thick lashes.

"Here's to no more fires in the kitchen tonight," he said lightly, watching her. "May they all be restrained to the bedroom—unless I can't wait and take you here on the table."

"Not on top of dinner!" Smiling at him, she felt her cheeks grow warm as she sipped the heady wine.

"Sit down and get off your foot," he said, pulling out a chair for her.

"All right, but first I want to call Renzi and tell him goodbye before it gets late and he goes to bed."

Ben handed her the phone and leaned down to kiss her. "Or before *you* go to bed," he drawled in a husky voice that made her tingle with anticipation.

She punched the preprogrammed one digit that rang the ranch and in minutes talked to Renzi until Ben set dinner in front of her. As she replaced the receiver, she wiped her eyes swiftly, struggling to keep from crying in front of Ben. He reached across the table and tilted her face up to study her.

"Let's eat before it gets cold," she said, not wanting sympathy. She put thoughts of leaving out of mind as she looked down at flaky white trout in a lemon dill sauce with newly made brown rice beside it. As soon as she bit into the fish, she glanced at him.

"You really can cook."

"This is simple fare and I've been alone a lot of my adult life. Let's not talk about me. Tell me about your job."

"Accounting is pretty routine at Falcon and I work for George Webster."

"He's not one I know," Ben said, listening while she talked about her work and they ate.

When they finished eating, he continued to sit and talk to her, his long, jean-clad legs stretched out. Finally he stood. "I'm putting the dishes in the dishwasher. You sit right there because I'll have them done in no time."

"Yes, sir, Captain Falcon! You're good at giving orders."

He grinned and shrugged. "That's the most efficient way to get this done."

She enjoyed watching him, feeling she could never get enough of looking at him. He moved with ease, his shirt stretching tightly across his shoulders as he reached for things or put dishes away.

The phone rang and Ben picked it up. The moment he frowned, she suspected it was Weston.

"She's right here." He handed her the receiver and moved away.

"Jennifer?"

"Yes," she said, hearing Weston's deep voice and picturing him and wondering how her life had become so complicated so swiftly.

"I got your message that you'll be flying in tomorrow night. I'll meet your plane."

"Thanks."

"Is Ben coming with you?"

"No. Sorry."

Silence stretched and she saw Ben glance at her. Finally Weston spoke. "Try to reason with him one more time, Jennifer. Just promise me that."

"All right, I will," she said, knowing it would do little good. She watched Ben squat down to get something from a cabinet, his jeans pulling tautly on his legs and she remembered him without the jeans or shirt.

"Do your best. When your plane gets in, I'll be there. I know you did what you could."

"Goodbye," she said, replacing the receiver.

"He's finally accepting things," Ben remarked. She noticed the hardness was back in his voice and she felt the world intruding on the happiness that had enveloped her for the past few hours.

"Yes, he is."

Ben crossed the room to rest his hands on her shoulders. "I'll tell you something about Weston if you don't know it already—he doesn't accept defeat. He doesn't give up trying to get his way."

She saw the muscle working in his jaw and wondered if the phone call had been an intrusion that he hated. "Ben, have you considered that he might have mellowed and changed with marrying Callie and then with losing her?"

"No man can mellow that much. Weston is ruthless."

She felt the barriers coming back up between them and she turned away, wanting to hold back arguments for the last night she would have with him.

Ben studied her, looking at the curtain of silky hair that fell over her shoulders and down her back, remembering how it felt across his bare chest and on his stomach and his legs.

The phone rang again and he wanted to swear, wondering if it would be Weston with some other strategy for talking him into coming back. Instead when he answered, Ben heard a deep voice and he grinned. He turned to Jennifer and held out the phone.

"Here's your teen admirer," he whispered with his hand over the mouthpiece.

"Todd?" She took the phone and Ben moved away to replenish Fella's dog dish and take care of household chores, because he suspected Todd had discovered Jennifer was leaving and his conversation would not be short.

Thirty minutes later, Ben had a roaring fire in the living room. He was seated on the sofa watching the flames dance up the chimney and thinking about going to Texas with her.

"I'm off the phone now. Todd says he's coming to Dallas someday to see me. I hope he outgrows this. I tried to be very impersonal with him."

"Darlin', you can't imagine the effect you have on males," Ben drawled as she walked to the sofa. She gave him a look while he pulled her down onto his lap. He wound a lock of her hair in his fingers. She looked at his thick lashes and dark eyes.

"Jennifer, I've thought about Weston and what you want. I'll go back with you tomorrow and see him."

Her heart missed a beat while she wondered whether she had heard him correctly. "You'll go back to Texas?"

He framed her face with his hands, his dark eyes going over her features and for an instant she forgot everything except Ben. Her gaze lowered to his mouth—the full underlip that was so sensual—and all she could think about was that she wouldn't be telling him goodbye tomorrow.

"I'll visit awhile and then I'm coming home."

"Oh, Ben!" She threw her arms around him, feeling as if she had won a major battle when she knew that it was only the most temporary and partial victory. "That's enough," she said, tears stinging her eyes. She was relieved and felt as if he were doing this for her, not Weston, and that touched her even more. She thought of the scars that laced Ben's back, scars that were even more terrible because they had been inflicted on him as a child. She knew that the Weston who had done that to his son had lost all right to expect his son to come home and take over a business.

"Tears?" Ben asked, running his thumb over her cheek.

"I'm just crying because I'm glad and because I think you're doing this for me."

"Damn straight, I am," he exclaimed. Her gaze met his and she felt her pulse jump. Worry was gone as Ben lowered his head to kiss her, twisting his long body and pulling her on top of him as he stretched out on the sofa. In minutes their clothes were scattered while they lay on the rug in front of the fire.

Jennifer pushed him down, sliding over him and turning him over to straddle him, her knees on either side of his waist. She ran her fingers over the scars and then leaned down to trail her tongue over his back, trying to avoid thinking about him as a child and bearing all of Weston's rage. She leaned over him, the tips of her breasts brushing his back. "Ben, I know you'd be a good father," she said, thinking about Ben's own experience and about Renzi.

Ben turned over, his dark eyes boring into her. "I was thinking about your worry over Renzi," she said, suddenly embarrassed that he might have misconstrued and thought she was making some oblique reference to marriage.

His hands ran over her breasts, his hungry gaze following his touch, and she forgot his worries. He cupped her breasts, flicking his thumbs over her nipples. "Do you like that?" he asked hoarsely.

She couldn't answer, closing her eyes and tilting back her head. His strong hands held her hips and shifted her, lifting her slightly and then pulling her down as he settled her on his hard erection.

The moment he filled her, she gasped with pleasure, feeling his hands on her nipples again and then one hand between her legs stroking her.

''Ride me, Jenny,'' he urged in a husky rasp, and she moved, urgency gripping her as his fingers and thick shaft drove her wild.

Ben watched her, trying to hold back, feeling sweat pour off him. She flung her head from side to side, the auburn hair swaying, and he wished he could make her his own, bind her to him, in some way that severed all ties she had in Texas. She was a fire in his blood, passionate, beautiful, all woman with a woman's warmth and giving.

Enveloped in rapture, Jennifer cried out with release while he held her, still impaled as he moved in hard thrusts to the rhythm of his own climax. Then she collapsed on him, her breasts against his bare chest, her hair spilling over him, both of them gasping for breath.

It was hours later when he carried her to the bed and far into the night before they both fell into sleep from exhaustion, Ben's arms tightly around her.

The next morning, she showered alone and dressed, a thread of joy and excitement running through her because Ben was going with her. Even though it was only a temporary visit, it changed their relationship because he was doing it for her.

Would it be an emotional battle when the two men were together? She fastened her hair behind her head with a ribbon, remembering the moment Ben had taken her barrette from her hair and tossed it away.

When she entered the kitchen, her pulse began the familiar drumming that the mere sight of him always caused. He was dressed in jeans and a work shirt and he looked ruggedly appealing. As she looked at him, she remembered his hands and mouth on her the night before.

"Morning," he drawled easily. He wrapped her in his embrace and kissed her, the welcoming kiss changing swiftly to a heated foray until she pushed against his chest. He felt warm and solid and she wanted his loving as much as before.

He gazed down at her while he still held her. "Will you come back up here sometime?"

Her heart thudded as she looked up at him and wondered how much the past few days had meant to him. "Yes. You know I will," she said quietly and he started to lean down, pausing when she pushed against his chest.

"Just one more kiss," he urged, wondering when he had developed this insatiable sex drive. "I'll get my work done."

It was more than one kiss until she moved away from him and they ate toast and drank orange juice and Ben left in long strides, heading for the barn to talk to Zeb.

Late that afternoon during the drive to Albuquerque, they talked and she learned more about his hopes for the ranch and his plans to enlarge his house if he adopted Renzi. As she talked to Ben, she sat sideways, studying him, her hand on his thigh covered by his hand much of the time.

By five o'clock they were airborne and as they flew across New Mexico and over Texas, she could feel the change coming over Ben. He became quiet, his jaw set; the hard look in his eyes that he had always had when she first met him was back. She felt nervous because even with the phone call in the airport to tell Weston that he need not meet them, the two were at cross-purposes.

The plane touched down and in minutes they strode through the walkway and then she spotted Weston in his navy pin-striped suit. He'd obviously decided to meet them even though she'd told him not to. She glanced at Ben, thinking he didn't look much like his father—he was more handsome with his rugged looks and raven hair. In his white Stetson, Western-cut clothes, a dark jacket and white shirt and jeans, he looked a rancher, self-assurance showing in the way he walked as much as it showed in Weston's stride. Here, Ben was at her side in Dallas—a marvel that had seemed impossible only yesterday.

Was there a chance he would stay?

Nine

Weston hugged Jennifer lightly and then when he turned to shake hands with Ben, Jennifer thought if strangers noticed them, they would assume it was a happy reunion. Unless someone looked into Ben's eyes. Weston clapped him on the shoulder.

"Ranching agrees with you. You're looking fit. Come on and Terry will get your bags. I brought Falcon's limo so we can talk. And you're both staying at the house. I've had clearance from Doc Gramercy for guests, so let's not waste time arguing."

They headed toward the front of the airport with Jennifer between the two men, Ben with a brown carryon over his shoulder.

"How's your foot?" Weston asked her.

"Better now," she answered, amazed that Ben had acquiesced easily to staying at Weston's. "I can stay at my apartment—"

"No arguments tonight," Weston replied firmly. "Jordan and his wife are waiting at the house. Tomorrow night we're having a dinner party so some of the men you worked with can say hello," he told Ben, who nodded, and she relaxed slightly because the first meeting had not been explosive.

In a short time Weston's stocky chauffeur, Terry, had the luggage loaded and was behind the wheel, pulling onto the freeway to drive through Dallas to an older part of town. They drove along wide streets with landscaped lawns and elegant homes set back from the street. Terry turned between tall wrought-iron gates and wound up a gravel drive. Ben climbed out, barely glancing at the mansion of white granite.

"Jordan's in the family room. Terry can take your things upstairs. Ben, I've put you in the west wing. He'll show you," Weston said to them as they entered a glassed-in porch that led into a large yellow-and-navy kitchen with ash cabinets. "Jennifer, we're doing over your old room, so Terry will show you where you'll be staying temporarily. I'll tell Jordan and Ila that you'll be down shortly."

Ben glanced around, seeing changes in decor, not caring, fighting a bristling feeling and hating the tight knot in his stomach that Weston always caused. As they entered the house, he looked at Weston, seeing the loose fit of his shirt around his neck, realizing Weston had lost some weight, but he looked tan and fit and not the invalid that Ben thought he might find.

They followed Terry up a wide, winding staircase covered in thick white carpet to the second floor where they turned down the hall to the west wing. Soft lights shone on the oil paintings decorating the walls and potted plants stood at intervals, but in spite of the decor, the house seemed as cold as ever to Ben. In minutes Terry motioned to a door.

"Miss Falcon, you're in here," he said, disappearing through an open door. She glanced at Ben who winked at

her and she smiled in return, suddenly stepping close to him
and standing on tiptoe to brush his cheek with a kiss.

He wanted to hold her and really kiss her, but he kept his
hands to himself while she followed Terry. When Terry
reappeared, he motioned to an open door across the hall.
"Mr. Ben, you're in here."

"Thanks, Terry. I can handle the bags." He took them
from the chauffeur and entered a large sitting room that
opened onto a bedroom. The decor was white and muted
shades of blue with provincial fruitwood furniture. Ben
crossed the room to the windows and looked down at a
lighted pool that was big enough for an Olympic swim meet.

Jennifer's door stood open and he rapped lightly, entering as he knocked. She was unpacking and looked up. He
closed the door behind him and watched her lower the shirt
she was holding. He had a dim awareness of another white
room with pink decor, but his attention was on her as he
crossed the room to her. He pulled her into his arms and
leaned down to kiss her hard, wanting to reassure himself
about her fiery response, wondering how much she would
change under Weston's spell. With his heart hammering,
Ben pulled her close.

The moment his tongue entered her mouth, she melted
against him, her tongue playing over his and arousing him
swiftly. His arms tightened around her while he forgot where
they were and kissed her until she pushed against him.

"They'll be expecting us downstairs. And I'll look like
I've been kissed. It's been hours since you shaved."

He grinned at her, rubbing her cheek with his. "Weston
won't object to my kissing you."

"What makes you think that?" she asked, her green eyes
widening.

He glanced at the room and waved his hand. "He put us
off to ourselves in this wing right across the hall from each
other. I know my father well enough to decipher his mach-
inations."

"Why would he want us to fall in love?" she asked, sounding so surprised at the thought that Ben's grin widened.

"Because you'd be the most luscious, sexiest, inducement for me to stay that he could provide."

"Ben Falcon, you're still accusing me of using my body to get you back here!" Her brows narrowed, and he found it was fun to tease her and get a firecracker reaction.

"Didn't you?" he asked, unable to resist and knowing that wasn't why she had succumbed to seduction.

"No!" She jabbed his chest with her forefinger. "That is the most infuriating, irritating, ridiculous—"

He laughed and kissed her, silencing her until she wriggled in his arms again and looked up at him breathlessly. "They're waiting downstairs. And I didn't use my body—"

"I know you didn't," he whispered in her ear, nuzzling her and flicking his tongue over her ear, "but you should have because we would have been here sooner."

"Ben!"

Chuckling, he released her. "Let's go greet old Jordan who would probably like to slip a dagger between my shoulder blades if he had half a chance."

"Unfortunately, I have to agree with you. I don't like Jordan. And Ila can barely tolerate me."

"My sneaky cousin will act civilized though. So will his wife as long as everyone's around."

Jennifer glanced at him and her eyes narrowed, but she didn't say anything and he didn't want to elaborate, remembering Ila offering herself to him once long ago. It had been at a party and he never knew whether it was out of spite toward Jordan or whether she slept around, but he got out of the situation and tried afterward to avoid being alone with her.

Ben took Jennifer's hand and they went downstairs, but before they entered the family room, he released her and walked in with a decorous distance between them, wanting to wait a while before letting Weston know about their relationship.

Ben glanced across the room at his tall cousin. He supposed women found Jordan handsome with his symmetrical features, large eyes, expressive mouth and thick blond hair. Even across the room, as Ben looked into Jordan's cold blue eyes, he could feel the hatred burn. He crossed the room to shake hands, receiving only the briefest shake.

"Welcome back to Texas," Jordan said with the enthusiasm of a snake viewing an alligator.

"It's been a long time," Ben replied easily as he turned to Ila, Jordan's wife, who had one brow cocked, her blue eyes watching him. Ila Falcon was a stunning woman with platinum blond hair and a voluptuous figure and clothes that cost Jordan dearly. Tonight she wore turquoise silk slacks and a silk shirt that had a V neck slashed to her waist and caught by one brass button that showed a tempting view when the silk parted.

"Ila," Ben said as she leaned forward to brush his cheek with a kiss and he caught a whiff of perfume.

"Welcome home, Ben. What a surprise to have you back."

"It's a surprise to me, too," he remarked, glancing around the room that was filled with antiques and oil paintings. His attention was caught by the large oil painting at one end of the room and he crossed the room to look at it. The woman bore a striking resemblance to Jennifer and he knew at once it was her mother. He wondered if Callie Falcon had been as beautiful a woman as she was portrayed by the painting. Her mass of red hair was like Jennifer's. The artist had captured a look in her deep green eyes that would make any man notice the picture. There was a faint smile on her face, a hint of passion in the clinging green silk dress that barely covered her breasts—the look of forbidden secrets locked forever in the silence of the picture. Ben became aware of Jennifer at his side.

"Your mother was a very beautiful woman."

"Yes, she was. And after marrying Weston, she became even more beautiful. She had an impact on men everywhere she went."

"I wondered why he married again after so many years. Now I think I know why."

"We should all drink to having Jennifer back with us and to her recovery after going off the mountain," Weston said behind them. When Ben turned, Weston handed him a glass of Scotch and soda. "Here's to a happy survival," Weston said, and they all raised their glasses in tribute to Jennifer who smiled in return.

"Tell us about it," Ila said.

Jennifer glanced at Ben. "Ben will have to tell you. I lost my memory for a few days."

Watching Jennifer, Ben told about finding her and the wreck. Gradually, conversation moved to discussing his ranch and cattle and then they went to dinner, but all the time Ben was barely aware of those around him as he watched Jennifer. She hadn't changed, still wearing her new blue woolen slacks and a blue silk blouse, her hair tied behind her head with a scarf. Since the return of her memory, there was a poise to her that he admired, always a hint of passion in the depths of her green eyes and he longed to be alone with her. He noticed Weston paid attention to everything she said, and he wondered if Weston was so taken with Jennifer because she reminded him of Callie.

The evening ended early and as soon as Ben showered, he yanked on jeans and crossed the hall to knock on Jennifer's door. Holding a green silk robe closed beneath her chin, she opened the door, gazing up at him and then stepping back when he entered. Without taking his gaze from hers, his pulse drumming and need building inside him, he closed the door and reached out to tug the sash free. Ben's fingers brushed her warm shoulders as he pushed the robe away, and it fell to the floor in a shimmering mass. She wasn't wearing anything beneath it, and his heart hammered against his rib cage. His erection was swift and hard as he wrapped his arms around her, picked her up and carried her to bed.

Later that night Ben lay staring into the dark while Jennifer slept curled against him in his arms. He wound a silky lock of her hair around his fingers. He needed her—needed her warmth, her company, her joy. They hadn't known each other a long time, yet looking back, his life seemed unimportant until she came into it. His life had been empty for a damned long time, yet in spite of the isolation and loneliness, he had never met anyone he wanted to come home to night after night. Now the thought of going back to the ranch without her tore at him.

But if the only way he could have her was to stay here in Texas to marry her, he couldn't do it. He looked down at her, her head nestled against his shoulder, her arm wrapped around him and he wanted her again, but he wanted more than just a few nights with her. He wanted forever.

His gaze swept the white room, moonlight spilling through the long windows over the opulent furnishings. He couldn't come back here to live. There was nothing for him here. Would she give this up for the ranch?

He was astounded by the feelings she evoked in him, beginning to understand for the first time how Weston might have mellowed because of Callie. A woman like Jennifer, with her softness and warmth, was enough to mellow the hardest of men.

Ben turned on his side, overwhelmed by his intense need for her, determined he wouldn't lose her. He wanted her to go home with him—to stay. It was the first time in his life he had considered a forever commitment. And yet he knew what he wanted—marriage. He kissed her temple lightly, remembering her with Renzi, smiling ruefully in the darkness at the thought that soon he might acquire a wife and a

child when a year ago he would have said that would be un-
likely for years—if ever.

He stroked her with his hand, feeling her warm smooth
skin as he pushed down the sheet and followed the curve of
her hip and then let his hand slide up her thigh, over her flat
belly, up to her breast to caress her nipple.

Tousled and asleep, she moaned and shifted. He was
hard, ready, wanting to enter her, but waiting to wake her.
He rubbed her nipple with his palm, watching her stir, feeling the hard bud that was erotically taut against his palm.

She rolled over, her eyes slowly opening. He shifted to kiss
her breasts and then moved between her legs, his tongue a
trail of fire until she gasped and shifted beneath him, opening for him. She wound her slender arms around his neck,
pulling him down as he entered her.

The next day, dressed in a charcoal-gray suit he hadn't
worn for over a year, he drove to the tall glass-and-steel
building that was the headquarters of Falcon Enterprises,
Incorporated. Water splashed in a fountain reflecting bright
sunshine before revolving doors. Inside the lobby was a large
bronze of a cowboy on a horse—a tribute to Weston's
ranching days, Ben supposed. Weston showed him around
for an hour and then Mark Kisiel, an engineering friend
from Ben's days with the company, took over the tour.
Once, Ben glimpsed Jennifer working, bent over a desk, her
hair neatly secured behind her head in a twist, her navy suit
jacket open.

The company had grown in the past eight years; the pro-
jects and accomplishments were impressive. But as he stood
in Mark's office and tried to pay attention, Ben felt closed
in and longed for the ranch.

That night was the dinner party with twenty Falcon executives and their wives. Ben wore the charcoal-gray suit. As
he stood in the living room sipping a drink while talking to

three of the men who worked for his father, his attention was caught by Jennifer when she entered the room.

It was the first time he had seen her in a dress and heels, and he felt as if someone had punched him in the middle. All the breath went out of his lungs and he didn't hear a word said by anyone around him.

"Excuse me," he mumbled, moving away from the men, knowing he was acting idiotic, but unable to take his gaze from her.

Her hair was piled high, looped and fastened on top of her head. She wore some kind of green dress—he had no idea the material, but it clung to her figure and the narrow skirt had a slit in front that revealed her long legs. She wore green pumps and looked as if nothing had happened to her ankle.

He paused in front of her and leaned down so he could whisper to her. "God, you're gorgeous!"

She smiled, dimple flashing and her eyes sparkling. "Ben! People will hear you."

"I don't give a damn. I'll announce—"

"Ben! You'll do no such thing," she said, squeezing his arm.

He grinned at her, wanting to whisk her back upstairs and remove the sexy dress. "How's your foot?"

"Right now, it's all right. If it starts to hurt, I'll put on slippers."

"If you do, come get me and let me help you put them on."

"I know how much you'll help me put something *on,*" she whispered, leaning close to him and giving him a heated look that made him draw a breath.

"Stop that, Jenny, or I'll have to leave the room because I'll have a condition that will embarrass us both."

"At your age? My goodness! If you get that way just talking about putting slippers on my feet, what would it do to you to talk about taking off my—"

"Jenny," he said, taking her arm and turning to walk outside on the wide veranda where cool breezes played over them. "I'll get revenge when we get upstairs."

"That sounds promising," she drawled in a sultry voice and he wanted to toss his drink into the garden, pick her up and carry her off to the gazebo that he knew was hidden on the grounds.

"One more remark like that from you and I'm going to give in to my baser impulses."

She rubbed her hip against him in a slow, sensuous movement that made him think very sensual thoughts. "Darlin', I didn't know you had base impulses."

"That does it!"

She stepped back and laughed. "You'll have to catch me later, hon," she said, slanting him a look over her shoulder that really did make him want to grab her. Another step and she turned again. "Oh, I almost forgot to tell you. I had an appointment with the doctor today. Now I'm protected."

Before he could answer, she stepped through the door and disappeared back into the house. Surprised, he stared after her, wondering if she was ready now for a long-term relationship. Lord knows, he was, even though it surprised him every time he thought about it. And he was seeing another tempting side to her, a provocative, relaxed side that he liked.

He walked to the edge of the veranda and looked at the riotous roses blooming in shades from purple to red. Letting his body cool down, he waited, grinning suddenly over the past few minutes with her because she was fun as well as warm and companionable. And fire in his arms in bed. He swore softly and tried to shift his thoughts away from bed and Jennifer.

The party lasted until eleven and then people said their goodbyes. Ben had promised a game of golf with friends, wondering if he could still hit the ball, it had been so long.

Finally they told Weston good-night and they were alone. As they went upstairs, Ben felt grateful to his father for putting the two of them in a separate wing of the house where he could have private moments with her and nights of love.

The next morning he returned to the Falcon offices to continue familiarizing himself with the business, going through the motions for Jennifer's sake and to see exactly how much he was needed.

Midmorning, Ben phoned Garrick Sutherland, another friend from earlier times. Before he hung up the phone, he agreed to lunch with Garrick the next day.

That afternoon Jennifer showed him her office on the fifth floor where the accounting department offices were located. She was in a large front room.

"I have my own office now."

He touched her nose, his gaze going over her features. "I'm not surprised since you're the boss's daughter."

She stuck her tongue out at him and both of them smiled and he wished again that he was alone with her.

"I better get back to work now, and you can continue your tour or whatever it is you're doing."

"Actually, I'd like to find a broom closet and shut you in it with me for about ten minutes."

"What did you have in mind?"

He leaned close to her ear and whispered just *exactly* what he would like to do, making her push him away. "Lord, I hope no one heard you! You've got a one-track mind."

"I do where you're concerned." He winked and left, taking the elevator to the sixth floor where the engineers' and geologists' offices were located.

The following day at noon, he sat across from his friend, studying Garrick's shaggy brown hair, his twinkling blue eyes, and his slightly crooked nose that was covered with freckles. "You don't look a day older, and it's been eight years."

Garrick grinned and shrugged broad shoulders covered by a plaid shirt that was tucked into khakis.

"And frankly, you don't look like one of the most successful men in America," Ben added with good nature.

"I leave the suits to the other guys if I can help it. Besides, I'm operating on Dad's money. Old money can be weird."

"How's it going?"

"Great. Are you coming back to work here?"

"No. I came back to see how Weston is faring. He had a heart attack a while ago."

"He had a mild heart attack and from what I hear he's doing fine. And the best thing in his life is his adopted daughter. If I knew your father wouldn't meddle in her life, I would have asked your stepsister out long ago."

"You're too damned late, I hope."

Garrick arched his dark brows and then laughed. "You—in love? That's as likely as Weston giving away his company."

"The lady's nice."

The waiter arrived with their food and Garrick studied Ben. "So, when are you buying a house?"

Ben lowered his glass of water and shook his head. "I'm not house hunting. I'm just here to see how Weston is, and then I'm going home."

"You're sure he can't talk you into coming back into the business?"

"No. Not now, not ever." Ben studied Garrick. "That wasn't an idle question, was it? You're considering a takeover?"

Garrick gave a wry smile. "You're too damned quick or you know me too well. I'm not admitting to anything, but I wanted to know if you would get hurt."

"No, but you'll never succeed. My father would kill to save his company. You don't know how obsessed he can be."

"Right now it's pure speculation," Mark said offhandedly.

Ben made a mental note to check with Mark Kisiel. When lunch was over, Ben shook hands with Garrick and drove back to Falcon Enterprises, mulling over Garrick's opinion that Weston was fine.

The rest of the week was busy, with Weston staying in the background while various officers of the company took Ben on tours, explained new acquisitions to him, showed him the books. Through all of it, Ben was aware Weston was staying home most of the time. Jordan avoided him, but during their few encounters, Ben could feel the tension and anger and knew Jordan wanted him to pack and go back to New Mexico.

Every night they went to parties or had company and after years in isolation on his ranch with little social activity, Ben found the parties wearing and he longed to get home, but he would give Weston time.

The first day in Dallas, he had called Weston's cardiologist and made an appointment to see him. On Friday, the second week of his visit, as soon as his enlightening talk with the physician ended, Ben drove to the Falcon offices, determined to relate to Jennifer that Weston wasn't as ill as he wanted everyone to think he was. He had a lunch date with Jennifer, but it was an hour away. He had free access to anything he wanted, so he headed for the geologists to see if one was in to talk about offshore holdings.

At ten minutes until twelve, he left Bart Thorkleson and rode the elevator down one floor. As he stepped into the hallway, he saw Jennifer ahead. She wore a red suit and with each step, her hips swayed seductively. He hurried to get closer behind her and let out a low whistle.

Frowning, she glanced over her shoulder and then shook her head. "I should have known!"

"My, I was enjoying the view. I had to show my appreciation. How about lunch in a hotel room around the corner?"

She laughed. "Not when I have to get back to work. Just a minute. I want to put this away."

"Take your time," he said, placing his hands on his hips. "You can come with me."

"You go ahead. I'll watch."

"Ben! Did you have all those lascivious thoughts when I first met you?"

He leaned closer to her. "You can't imagine how lusty my thoughts were then. When I had to undress you—"

"Stop right there," she said in mock alarm, "before someone hears you! We'll finish this discussion tonight."

"That hotel room for lunch still sounds good to me."

"Absolutely not! I have some work to get done and in the mail by three this afternoon. One hour for lunch is all. Not a minute over."

"Yes, ma'am," he said. She gave him a dimpled smile and turned to go down the hall. He moved to the side of the hallway and leaned his shoulder against the wall. Hooking his thumb into his belt, he watched her walk away from him and mentally stripped away the red suit. She turned to enter her work area, looked down the hall at him and slanted him a look that made his temperature rise before she disappeared from sight.

Thirty minutes later, as they sat in the glassed-in busy restaurant, she lowered her fork to her plate, frowning at him.

"That isn't what I was told," she said.

"I spent an hour this morning with his cardiologist. Stuart Neale said Weston is doing nicely. He can go to work if he doesn't overdo it. He's supposed to walk and get exercise."

"I talked to Stan Gramercy—the family doctor—and he said Dr. Neale said Weston was to cut back, to take it easy and retire."

Ben leaned closer over the table. "Stan is a close friend of Weston's, on his payroll because Falcon employees see Stan. He will say what Weston wants him to say."

"I don't believe you!"

Ben shrugged. "Talk to Neale yourself."

"Why would Weston do such a thing? He's never wanted to step down or take it easy, but if he wanted to, he could have at any time without getting Stan to say he had to. That doesn't make sense."

"Except there wouldn't have been as much argument to get me back if he had just said he wanted to retire. You would never have argued with me over that."

"I can't believe Stan would lie. That's unethical."

"Weston pays him well," Ben said dryly.

She glanced at her watch. "I have to get back."

Ben drank the last of his coffee and stood. He had already paid the bill and he took Jennifer's arm. In the car she opened a small notebook and made a notation, and he studied her. All through lunch until he brought up the talk with Weston's doctor, she had seemed to hum with excitement and he realized she loved what she was doing. "You like your work, don't you?"

"I love it," she said, closing the notebook and slipping it into her purse. "Falcon Enterprises is growing every month and I'm part of that."

Her green eyes sparkled with eagerness and he felt another tug of doubt. He had spent long hours the past week in jewelry stores and he had purchased a ring. Now as he watched her, he wondered if she would leave her job. He turned into the Falcon Enterprises lot and slowed in front of the wide glass doors. "Pick you up at five?"

"Better call first. I may be late tonight."

"Sure, hon."

She flashed him another dimpled smile and he slipped his hand behind her neck to pull her to him to kiss her long and hard, feeling as if he wanted to drive thoughts of business and numbers out of her mind. When she opened her eyes, she seemed to take a minute to focus on him.

"Thanks for lunch," she said in a breathless voice that made him feel better.

"That's nothing. Wait until dinner—it's Friday night and we're going dancing."

"Oh, my," she said, touching his cheek and then leaning forward to brush a kiss across his lips. "And I have a surprise for you tonight."

Curious, he studied her. "Now I'll be trying to guess what it is all afternoon."

"That'll keep you thinking about me."

"Hon, if you knew how much and what I'm thinking—"

She laughed. "Stop right there or I'll never get back to work." She turned, her hand resting on the door handle. "Here comes Jordan. Thanks, Ben." She stepped out and closed the door. As she walked toward the building, Jordan spoke to her and then came around the car to lean down at Ben's open window.

"Are we going to have a wedding soon?"

"No, Jordan. If we do you'll know about it."

"That's all it would take to put you right back in solidly with your father."

"Jordan, not in the next million years will I be back in solidly with him. And marriage to Jennifer wouldn't do it."

"Why do I doubt that?" Jordan stepped away from the car, his blue eyes glittering with malice as Ben drove away without looking back.

When he reached Weston's house, Ben shut himself in his room and called home to check on any messages and discovered Derek wanted to talk to him. He placed a call to the ranch and in minutes Derek's cheerful voice boomed.

"Glad you got my message. How's Dallas?"

"About like I expected. I'll be home soon."

"Not too soon for us. We have a faulty safety valve in the hot water tank."

"Go buy a new one and I'll install it when I get there."

"Ben, that isn't why I called you," he said, his voice changing and sounding earnest. "Eloise Lopez is putting Renzi up for adoption."

Ben's pulse jumped and he gripped the phone, closing his eyes as relief and joy poured through him. "It would be better for him if his mother took him back."

"Counselors have talked to her and she isn't going to. She has a doctor's statement that her nerves can't cope with a child at this point in her life. He either goes to a state agency or someone adopts him."

"I don't know how that woman can give him up, but I want to adopt him."

"Get your lawyer. She says she knows what she's doing. She's moving to Oregon with the new boyfriend. She could take Renzi if she wanted to, but she doesn't. I think once he's adopted, she'll marry again, but I don't think she wants a child clouding things."

"How much does Renzi know?"

"Nothing yet. I wanted to talk to you first, and you should be the one to tell him. She's not even coming up here to say goodbye to him."

"All right, I'll call my lawyer and we'll get started as quickly as possible. I'll be home Saturday or Sunday if it'll help."

"Good. Renzi's been asking about you and Jennifer. So has Todd—been asking about Jennifer, that is. I don't think Todd is quite so taken with you, no offense."

Still concerned with the adoption, Ben couldn't laugh. "I'm not going to sleep nights until I know about Renzi. How long does adoption take?"

"When you're not going through a lot of red tape, it doesn't have to take a long time, and this place isn't a state agency, so if you have a good lawyer, you should see things move right along. And the mother can't wait."

"God, that woman—"

"We won't tell Renzi until we know for certain. No use getting his hopes up. She has to sign papers, and the sooner the better, because if she leaves the state—"

"I'll call my attorney right now. Thanks, Derek."

"Take it easy, Ben. Give Jennifer a kiss for all of us."

"Yeah, sure," he said, listening to the phone click and looking at the line. He called his attorney and then moved to the window to stare outside. It was time to go home. And time to ask Jennifer if she would go with him. Tonight he was taking her dancing and he could talk to her then when there would be no interruptions. He looked at the luxurious room and it meant nothing to him. Home was the ranch in the mountains, not this place, but would she be willing to give this up?

"Sir," came a soft voice at the door, and he turned to see the maid, Darlene. "Your father wondered if you could step down to his office. He'd like to see you."

"Sure. Tell him I'll be there in just a few minutes."

He made another call to the ranch and then he went downstairs.

Ben entered the walnut-paneled office, glancing around at the room that he'd detested when he was young, because so often Weston had brought him here to reprimand him. It had been redecorated and refurnished since that time—in deep maroon leather furniture and polished mahogany furniture, a huge carved desk dominating the room.

Weston wore a white shirt and slacks and he sat on a recliner, his legs crossed, his head turned as he gazed out the window. When he heard Ben, he motioned to him to come in. Ben studied him, still surprised by the amount of gray in his father's brown hair.

He motioned to Ben. "Sit down. I appreciate your coming home and taking an interest again in Falcon when I need you."

Ben sat on a straight-back wing chair, his glance going beyond Weston to the windows and the well-tended grounds outside. Banks of white spirea bloomed like streaming fountains over a greening earth and he knew spring had come earlier to Dallas than to the mountains. His gaze came back to Weston.

"Since when did I become your fair-haired, favored son?" Ben asked, not making an effort to hide the sarcasm in his voice.

Weston's blue eyes met his steadfastly. "Since I realized how like me you really are."

"God, I hope not," Ben said quietly.

"See, even your reaction now—" He broke off and ran his fingers through his hair. It sprang back and Ben looked at Weston's thick fingers and recalled the pain they could inflict. "I'm tired of Jordan constantly saying yes to me. I need someone who can think independently."

"I doubt if he said yes to you when you told him you were sending Jennifer for me."

Weston turned to focus on Ben and gave a small chuckle. "No, he sure as hell didn't. Jordan's a smart man and he's done a good job, but I need more than that."

Ben thought of the times Weston had listened to Jordan, turning a deaf ear to his own sons. Five years older than Ben, Jordan had set up Ben many times as a child, getting him into trouble.

"You're in love with Jennifer, aren't you?"

"Yes," Ben answered.

"And she's in love with you. She's young and inexperienced. I hope you don't hurt her."

"I don't intend to."

"Her mother was the most beautiful woman to ever walk the earth. My years with her were the happiest." Weston's blue eyes focused on Ben intently. "I need you to come back to work here." Weston leaned forward slightly. "You're the strong man, not Jordan. Jordan can run our company, but he'll never make it a giant conglomerate, never do what you can do."

"Well, I'll be damned," Ben said, his edginess evaporating in the wake of stunned surprise. "All my life," he said carefully, "while I was growing up, and too many years afterward, I tried to live up to you and become a son you would be proud of. And I never could. Never. This is the first time in my life that I can recall anything complimentary about me from you and it's coming too late. I'm like Scarlett—frankly, Father, I don't give a damn." And silently, Ben promised himself, if he got to adopt Renzi, he would tell Renzi every day that he loved him and he would try to remember to praise any achievement Renzi made. "Too bad you didn't realize my potential when I worked for you," Ben added dryly.

"You were younger, and I didn't need you and wasn't ready for you to take charge." Weston moved impatiently, a familiar hard note coming to his voice.

"I don't recall ever trying to take charge. I just remember trying to make some business decisions."

"That's all in the past."

"You don't need me now. I talked to Dr. Neale."

"Anything concerning me is confidential—he couldn't have told you anything."

"I convinced him that, as your son and next of kin, I needed to know some things, make some plans."

Weston's jaw firmed and Ben saw the blaze of anger in his eyes, but it was banked the moment it flared. "Come back to work for me now. If you'll come back," Weston began, placing his hands on his hips and Ben wondered how big the bribe would be this time. "If you'll step in now, I'll make you president of Falcon Enterprises. I'll remain CEO, but I won't work as often and I'll turn the business over to you more and more. You'll be over Jordan.''

''You'd give Jordan apoplexy.''

''He would adjust,'' Weston answered flatly. ''You'll make enough money that you can hire someone competent to run your ranch. In addition, I'll rewrite my will. Currently, you're not included in it except for the token dollar. I'll change that so my estate is divided three ways, to you, to Jennifer and to Jordan. You'll become head of Falcon Enterprises.''

Ben shifted and then stood, restlessly crossing the room to the window, thinking of the offer and all he would have. He looked at the antiques in the room, the collector's furniture. He would have what most men could only dream about.

''And Jennifer would be part of this,'' Weston reminded him. ''Imagine the times you could have with her and all you could give her. Between the two of you, you would have two-thirds of my estate.''

Ben thought of his small ranch house, the rugged life, the harsh winters and the isolation. He looked around the room again, thinking of Weston's far-flung holdings, the ranch, the stable of fine quarter horses, the company jet.

''Jennifer told me about the boys' ranch,'' Weston continued quietly. ''If you accept my offer, imagine what you can give them—new buildings, money, equipment—things they'd never have otherwise.''

For a second Ben closed his eyes. How like Weston to put the most temptation possible in front of him. Ben turned around to face his father and he could remember the beatings, the rage Weston had vented on him when he had been small and Weston had looked like a giant. And Weston wasn't stepping down. He met Weston's gaze and he raised his arm, giving a little pull so his cuff slipped away from his wrist, revealing the burn scar on the inside of his wrist.

''I don't think I was five years old,'' he said quietly.

"That's past, Ben. Don't throw away your future because I was too harsh on you as a child. You were a rebellious child. And don't throw away Jennifer's future."

"To hell with that," Ben said quietly. "Up until a certain point in my life I loved you because children want to love their parents. You drove every last shred of that love out of me. I don't believe your offer—"

"I'll draw up a will tonight."

"I believe the inheritance. I don't believe you'll relinquish control of the business for years. I just told you, I talked to your cardiologist and you're able to go to work. And all you've told Jennifer is so much crap."

"All right, I am. But the attack made me think about the future and realize I'm not immortal. Falcon Enterprises is my only son right now. This company is all I really have. I've heard rumors about a hostile takeover of Falcon. You can help me fight the sharks off. And then I want to make certain this company grows into the powerful business I think it can and you're the only Falcon who can come in and take charge and see to it that it does."

"Ah, it has to be blood relation to take charge."

"Yes. No one else will care as much. And you're the only one who is man enough, tough enough and intelligent enough to do it. Will you do it?"

Once again, Ben was shocked by Weston's opinion of him. "Your confidence in me comes eight years too late."

"Don't be a jackass over old grudges and throw away an absolute fortune and the most challenging and rewarding career possible. You take this offer and you can have anything in life you want—power, political office..."

Ben gazed into Weston's blue eyes and felt the old pull between them, the differences, the clash that would never end. If he moved back, how long would Weston sit on the sidelines once Ben had rearranged his life? Ben thought about his ranch, the clear mountain streams, the smell of pine and spruce, Renzi's dark eyes, and he knew what he wanted.

"Thanks for the offer and the belated high opinion, but I'm leaving, Weston. I'm going to ask Jennifer to marry me and I'm going home to New Mexico."

Ten

"**D**on't be a fool!" Weston yelled. "You can't turn this offer down."

"I just did," Ben said quietly, shaking his head. "I don't want to move back here. I don't give a damn about Falcon Enterprises. I don't want to work with Jordan. He hates my guts. You can almost feel it when we're in the same room."

"Jordan will do what is necessary. Are you really thinking about what you're throwing away here?" Weston snapped, his temper rising as he stood.

"Now you're getting more like your old self, the father I know," Ben said. "I came close to hitting you once when I was a teenager."

"If you had, I would have killed you," Weston said. "You're smart, dammit, too smart to throw all this away. What have you got now? A stinking little ranch I could buy tomorrow."

"No, you can't because it's not for sale."

"I imagine I can find a price or a way to ruin you."

"Now we've gone from promises and bribes to threats—an old pattern, Weston."

"You're not taking Jennifer."

"I think that's the lady's choice, not yours," Ben remarked.

Weston shook his head while he placed his hands on his hips. "If you turn me down and ask her to marry you and go back with you, you don't really love her," Weston declared emphatically, his words giving Ben a jolt. "She likes her job. This morning I offered her a position as vice president of accounting with Falcon—she wanted to surprise you tonight."

Ben felt a tightening in the pit of his stomach because he remembered the times he had seen her enthusiasm and eagerness when she worked.

"If you turn me down," Weston continued, his eyes narrowing, "I'll change my will and she'll inherit half of everything I own—unless she's married to you." Weston's blue eyes burned with determination. "You can't give her anything like that," he said, and the sting of Weston's words hurt more than any physical blows Ben had ever received. "You can't give her fancy homes and a life of luxury and a career she adores. And if you love her, you won't take her away from all of that."

Ben felt as if Weston had slammed a fist into his gut because Weston was right, and Ben did love her.

"If you ask her to marry you," Weston said softly, "then you're asking for all the selfish reasons you accuse me of having. You won't be thinking of her welfare or her future."

Ben closed his eyes while pain knotted inside because he couldn't deny what Weston was saying. "Damn you," he said quietly, knowing Weston had won.

"You can have it all—and Jennifer," Weston said slyly, his voice cajoling. "All the money, the career, the beautiful woman who would adore you. Why the hell are you throwing that away for some two-bit ranch in New Mexico?''

Ben thought about the ranch and the daily challenges and he remembered working at Falcon, fighting with Jordan, the politics, dealing with Weston. And he knew Weston would not step down.

"Move back," Weston urged. "In three months you'll wonder why you hesitated. You're not a rebellious kid any longer, Ben."

Ben stirred restlessly, his hands on his hips while he thought about coming back. He would hate working with Jordan as much as Jordan would hate working with him. And if he married Jennifer and adopted Renzi, if they stayed here in Dallas, she wouldn't give up her job, and at the moment he wanted someone to be home for Renzi.

"No man can turn his back on what I'm offering," Weston said.

Ben looked at him, feeling the anger build inside because Weston was taking Jennifer from him with his promises and promotions and gifts. "I can," he answered. "I won't work for you again, Weston. It wouldn't be any different from last time. The first time I wanted to do something you didn't like, you'd step in." He studied his father, suddenly so certain of what he was saying. "I'll come back under one condition."

Weston's eyes narrowed. "What's that?"

"You sell your share of the company—you get out, off the board. You sever every tie you have with Falcon." Anger flared in Weston's eyes.

"You're the world's biggest fool, Ben," Weston answered, his deep voice almost a snarl, and Ben knew he was right about Weston's intentions.

"I didn't think you'd turn the power over to me," Ben said quietly.

"So your answer is no." Weston clenched his fists and his face darkened and Ben wondered if he would try to hit him.

"Then get out of my house. You're no longer my son. Get out now. And if you love Jennifer, for her sake, you'll never ask her to go with you."

Ben drew a deep breath and crossed the room, his stormy thoughts on Jennifer, knowing Weston was right. Ben swore under his breath. He loved her and he wouldn't ask her to give up everything Weston could offer her. He remembered her excitement at lunch, her enthusiasm for her job. And that was only a small part of what Weston would give her.

In long strides he left the room and took the stairs two at a time. At the top he glanced down. Looking ready to fight, Weston stood in the hallway. He turned and strode down the hall out of sight.

Ben tossed his things into the carryon, called a taxi, made reservations at a hotel and made plane reservations to go home—alone. He felt as if his heart had been ripped out. He wanted to go down to Falcon and pick up Jennifer and carry her out of her office to his hotel and ask her to marry him. But now he couldn't. He loved her and he wouldn't take the bounty and luxury and ease from her that Weston offered.

Thrusting the small box with the diamond ring into his pocket, he zipped up the carryon. When he stepped into the hall, he glanced at Jennifer's room. Hurting, he went downstairs and outside to see the cab turn into the drive.

He checked into the hotel, rented a car and drove to Falcon Enterprises. He looked at the steel-and-glass building that represented the power of the man who owned it. Clenching his fists, Ben entered the cool interior. He walked to the elevators and took one to Jennifer's floor, looking at the offices as he walked down the hall, considering again what it would be like to give up his ranch. The business was all Weston's and Jordan's, and Ben couldn't step back into it. And he couldn't ask Jennifer to give it up. Tonight was going to be the worst night of his life, but he had to tell her goodbye without letting her know the real reason. Then he had to get out of her life.

As he walked toward her desk, he drew a deep breath, feeling as if he were tied in knots inside.

Jennifer glanced around from the spreadsheet on her PC to see Ben standing in the doorway. "Hi. What are you doing here?"

When he entered the room, Jennifer looked into his stormy gaze and her breath caught. Dressed in his boots, jeans and a white shirt, his dark eyes flashed with anger, his expression was hard, his shoulders stiff. He thrust his hands into his pockets and crossed the room to stand on the other side of her desk. His dark gaze swept over her as if he wanted to devour her. "Can you get away?"

A cold feeling that something must be dreadfully wrong spread inside her. She nodded. "Have a seat and give me a minute."

Like a caged tiger, he paced the room and she hurried, making two calls, putting things away while she talked, shutting down the computer. Finally she grabbed her purse out of her desk drawer and yanked up her red suit jacket. "I'm ready."

He took her arm and they left the building in silence. When he led her to a black car, she wondered where he had gotten it, but didn't ask. As soon as he slid behind the wheel, he turned to look at her. "I talked to Weston today. He made me an offer, and I turned it down."

Jennifer could see the anger in Ben's gaze and there was a tightness in his voice that made her wonder what had happened between the two men. "You're so sure you don't want this?" she asked, feeling sadness and a sense of dread.

"I'm damn sure."

She closed her eyes for an instant, disappointed, even though she had expected that answer. "I was called in to see Jordan this morning and given a promotion to vice president of accounting," she said. The promotion that had dazzled her so much earlier now seemed far less important. With Ben tied to his ranch and her to her career, with trying to see each other when they lived in different states, their lives would be complicated.

"Congratulations," Ben said, his voice warming as he leaned forward to kiss her lightly. His lips brushed hers, and then he looked at her, an inscrutable stormy look that she didn't understand. Without speaking, his hand went behind her neck and he pulled her to him, holding her while his mouth covered hers and he kissed her hard and passionately.

Ben hurt all over and he wanted to hold her close and ask her to marry him. Instead, he leaned back a fraction. "I have a hotel room. Let's go there."

She frowned. "Hotel? Aren't you staying at the house?"

"When I turned down his offer, Weston told me to get out."

"Oh, Ben, was it so terrible?"

"Yes, it was," he said in what must have sounded like a snarl as he started the car again and drove out of the parking lot to his hotel. When he kicked the door of the room closed behind them, he wrapped Jennifer in his arms and bent over her to kiss her, feeling desperation tearing through him because he knew it was the last time he would get to hold and kiss and love her. He was going to walk out of her life and leave her to all of Weston's dazzling promises, but for this moment, Ben wanted to think she was his.

He wound his fingers in her hair and shook away pins that held it in a twist behind her head. Her fiery auburn locks tumbled over her shoulders and he buried his fingers in them, feeling the silkiness. With his other hand, his fingers twisted free the buttons on her blouse and pushed it away.

Her green eyes darkened with passion as her lips parted. Pushing away her white lace bra, his rough, tanned hand cupped her breasts, her softness filling his palm. As he thought about the ring that was in his suitcase, his throat tightened. He stepped back to unfasten her skirt, fighting the urgency that gripped him, wanting to take his time and savor every inch of her, memorizing textures and curves, wanting their loving to never end, yet knowing it was going to be all too final.

With his pulse pounding, Ben pushed the skirt over her hips and let it fall around her ankles. Her lush full breasts and tiny waist took his breath away. When she stepped out of her pumps, he peeled away the hose, revealing lacy red panties and his hands slid down over her legs, relishing their smoothness.

He straightened, his gaze drifting over her, and Jennifer's pulse pounded eagerly while she twisted free his buttons and pushed off his shirt. When her fingers went to his belt, he caught her hand. "Not yet," he said in a harsh voice, his stormy dark gaze meeting hers.

Startled, Jennifer drew a deep breath, suddenly realizing he was telling her goodbye. "You're leaving, aren't you?" she blurted, a fearsome, cold hurt uncurling inside her. Her head swam for a moment as she realized she had given her heart and he had kept his locked away and now he was going to tell her goodbye.

She could bear it if he turned down Weston; she had expected him to now that she knew Ben and knew about his relationship with his father. But looking into Ben's eyes, she realized that he was really leaving. He wasn't coming back and he wasn't going to ask her to the ranch.

"Ben." The word came out in a rush, longing swamping her as she wrapped her arms around his neck and kissed him, fitting her body against his hard length as if she could change his mind. His arms banded her, crushing her against him until she felt as if she couldn't get her breath, and he kissed her with as much desperation and hunger as she felt. Her heart pounded while she broke away to look up at him.

"Don't go. If you kiss me like that, you don't want to go," she said solemnly.

His breathing was ragged, and suddenly he picked her up and carried her to his bed. He yanked his belt and jeans free,

peeling away her panties with shaking hands, and then he
was poised over her, his dark eyes sweeping over her.

"Ben—"

He lowered himself, easing into her, his mouth covering
hers and stopping her question. She was lost in spiraling
sensation as his hard shaft filled her. She moved with him,
clinging to him, her hands holding his firm buttocks and her
legs wrapped tightly around him while she tried to make the
moment last, scared of what was ahead. And then all
thought vanished. "Ben! Ben, I love you!" she cried.

Ben fought to pleasure her as long as he possibly could
while her cry of love tore through him like a knife in his
heart. He wanted to tell her he loved her, to ask her to marry
him and go home with him. He couldn't do any of it. Her
soft warmth enveloped him, a flame searing him, driving
him to a frenzy until he forgot the pain and loss and was
consumed by her. Thrusting fiercely, he bit back a cry of
love as he climaxed, wanting to make her his forever and
knowing that she was slipping away from him even while his
body was joined with hers.

He held her tightly in his arms, stroking her, his thoughts
roiling, and when she twisted around to talk to him, he began loving her again, wanting her as if they had never made
love.

It became a night of desperate lovemaking and Jennifer
knew Ben didn't want to talk. Finally she fell into an exhausted sleep in his arms.

When she stirred the next morning, he had showered and
shaved and was moving around the room. He wore his jeans
that were still unbuttoned at the waist and for a moment she
forgot the night and any problems. He crossed the room to
kiss her.

"You have to dress," he said in a husky voice.

Suddenly she sat up. "Great grief! What day is it?"

"Saturday. You don't have to be at work, but I have to go to the airport and I want to take you home first. I'm not leaving you stranded here at the hotel."

She gazed at him solemnly because he was leaving her heart stranded. "When will you be back?"

"I'll call you," he said, and she knew he wouldn't. It hurt, an agonizing loss that would become terrible when he was gone. She tried to remind herself that he had never made promises, never said he loved her, never planned a future. Her heart had just charged ahead, falling in love with him, dancing on a high rope without a net below and now taking the fall. He glanced at his wristwatch. "My plane leaves at nine."

Not certain she could keep her emotions from sounding in her voice, she just nodded. He moved away, turning his back while he gathered his things and she went to shower and dress.

Twenty minutes later, he faced her at the door. "I'll call you, Jenny," he said in a husky voice, and reached out to kiss her one more time. His arms banded her tightly, pulling her against him while he bent over her, his tongue going deep, heat and longing filling her. Kissing him in return, she wanted to make him remember her, remember their kisses.

Finally he released her and they left, riding the elevator in silence. He drove swiftly along the empty freeway and too soon he stopped in front of Weston's house. Ben kissed her one more time and then opened the car door. "I'll call," he repeated, as if that was the only thing he knew to say.

She nodded and climbed out swiftly, terrified she would burst into tears in front of him. She stepped back, looking at him and then watched while he drove down the drive and into the street. She turned to go inside, not seeing the house that usually pleased her so much. To her relief no one stirred, and she went to her room, closing the door, wishing there was some way to stop the dreadful pain that she suspected she was going to live with for a long time.

At noon Weston rapped on her door and thrust his head inside. "Time for lunch."

"I don't feel well."

"Well, come keep me company and let's discuss your promotion," he said briskly. "You'll be surprised how much better you'll feel. C'mon."

"I'll be there in a minute." She washed her face with cold water. Her eyes and nose were still red even though she had stopped crying over an hour ago.

In the airy breakfast room, Weston had one of her favorites—Caesar salad with grilled chicken strips. He talked about what she could do in her new position, and if he seemed to notice she wasn't adding to the conversation, he gave no indication. "I suppose Ben's plane took off all right. I'm disappointed he turned me down, but I should have known he would never change. He couldn't wait to get back to his ranch. He said that's his only love and he wouldn't leave it for anyone or anything."

She couldn't get down the salad and she wanted to be alone, but it would be rude to leave just yet. Weston lowered his fork and studied her. "You're in love with him, aren't you?"

She looked up into Weston's blue eyes and clamped her lips together, knowing she didn't need to answer his question. He reached across the table to take her hand in his. "I'm sorry, Jennifer," he said gently. "You don't believe me, but you'll get over him. I've had two marriages, and time changes your perspective especially when you're young. You're inexperienced—the only other man you've dated was Devin, and you recovered easily enough from that. You'll forget Ben, too, and the pain you feel now will vanish and you'll laugh when you look back to think you ever felt this way."

"Maybe," she said, unable to believe that could possibly happen.

"I know." His voice lowered. "My son can't be tied down. Women in his life have always come and gone. Ben doesn't like commitments."

She studied her glass of ice water, hearing Weston, the words telling her what she already knew. He hadn't asked her to call or come see him—all he had done was say good-bye.

"Weston, excuse me," she said. "I need to get back to my apartment—"

"No. I've been through grief and loss, and to sit alone and agonize is not the way to get over it. I know you don't want to do anything, but you're going with me tonight to a jazz concert, and if the noise and raucous behavior doesn't drive some of the pain away for a few minutes, I'll be greatly surprised. And you're staying here for a few days. Tomorrow night, I'm having a dinner party to celebrate your promotion. I know you don't want to, but believe me, you'll look back later and be glad."

"I'd rather not," she said, really not caring what she did. "I won't be good company."

"You don't have to be. I have all sorts of fascinating people invited. I'll bet you lose your heart to one of them within a few months."

"Weston—"

"It's not that impossible. I didn't think I'd ever marry again, but when I met your mother, I loved her more than I've ever loved anyone," he said.

She nodded. "I'm going upstairs."

"Go have a good cry, but be ready to go at seven because I'm taking you to dinner. Jennifer—"

She glanced back at him. "Just remember—he's not crying. He's doing just what he damned well pleases regardless of whom he hurts."

She nodded and drew a deep breath, hurrying from the room, knowing that Ben had never given her promises and that she shouldn't be surprised that he was gone.

"Ben," she whispered, wondering how she would get through the next days, thinking she would never be able to concentrate on her work next week and wondering if a month from now the hurt would be just as great. "Ben," she repeated, glancing out the window.

Still keeping in touch with Renzi, she called him, crying while she talked to him, hearing his excitement that Ben was on his way home. With a promise to call the next week, she finally hung up.

During the next few weeks Weston kept her busy at night and she was busy at work, though she was making incredible mistakes and she knew it was because she couldn't concentrate. Days passed until a month was gone since she had kissed Ben goodbye. She talked less often to Renzi, and she hadn't talked once to Ben. Not once. As she sat at her desk, figures blurred in front of her and she wiped her eyes.

"Crying again?" came Jordan's voice, and he stepped into her office and closed the door, crossing the room to sit down across from her and smoothing his navy trousers over his knee.

She felt the cold dislike Jordan always caused and she was embarrassed to have him find her crying. He gazed at her with a faint smile. "You really don't have a lot to cry over," he said.

"Jordan, I have all this work—"

"And you're taking three hours to do things that used to take you one hour."

"Do you want me to quit?"

"Good Lord, no! I don't have authority over you. We're both vice presidents. I just don't know if you realize how fortunate you are. Or what he gave up."

She studied Jordan, knowing he could be sly and devious and wondering what he was up to now. He waited, and when she didn't speak, he continued, "Weston changed his will."

"I really am not interested—"

"You should be. He offered Ben one-third, you a third and me a third to stay. Ben turned him down. So now you'll inherit half and I'll inherit half of everything. You and I will be co-owners of Falcon Enterprises."

She stared at him in shock for a moment, completely taken aback. She had gone further now than she had ever dreamed possible, knowing that she was a vice president so swiftly because Weston had seen to it, but she never dreamed she would inherit half of his estate. "He cut Ben out completely?"

"Of course. He offered him the presidency of the company and all that would go with it, one-third of the estate, and obviously, if he had stayed, he could have had you."

She shot Jordan a glance. "What do you want, Jordan?"

"I wanted to tell you." He laughed ruefully. "I can't believe I'm doing this, but I've always admired you, Jennifer."

She stared at him, certain he was lying about always liking her. And then she realized if she went to New Mexico and Ben still loved her—it would leave only Jordan to run Falcon. If she married Ben, it would be typical of Weston to change his will again, and Jordan knew it. She didn't care what Jordan's motives were if he was telling her the truth. She tried to bring her attention back to him.

"You're suffering. Why do you think Ben went back to New Mexico without asking you to go with him?" Jordan stood. "I won't have to tell you. You're smart enough to figure out the rest."

She barely heard him, staring at the door as he closed it behind him, thinking about what Jordan had said.

Two days later she asked for a week's vacation and she began to get her work in order to go. Friday afternoon Jordan paused and rapped on her door before stepping into her office. He placed a briefcase on her desk. "Ben left this behind. It's some papers he collected while he was here. I was going to get my secretary to mail it to him, but then I thought if you're not taking too much..."

"Sure, I'll take it to him," she said, setting the briefcase on the floor beside the desk.

"I have a feeling this is goodbye," Jordan said. "Maybe we'll both be happier."

She laughed at his honest statement. "I have to go see for myself. But I may be back, Jordan."

He gave her a smile and left without another word.

Ben caught Renzi up in his arms as he left the courtroom. "You belong with me, now, kiddo."

Renzi hugged Ben's neck as Ben looked at Derek. "It seemed simple when it got right down to the actual legalities."

"A courtroom procedure and costs for you to pay. You'll come back and visit us, won't you, Lorenzo?"

"Sure." He grinned and wriggled and Ben set him down, watching him hurry ahead of them down the hall. He wore the new jeans Ben had bought and a plaid shirt, and Ben was awed to think Renzi was his son now.

"I can't believe I'm a father and he's my son."

Derek held out his hand. "Congratulations."

"Thanks."

"I still think you should call Jennifer and let her make her own decision."

Ben shook his head. "No. I haven't heard from her, and knowing Weston, he's keeping her so entertained and busy and moving her into a jet-setting life-style that she won't miss life in the mountains."

"She seemed to fit in here pretty damned good."

"Yeah," Ben answered, pushing open the door to the courthouse.

That night, while he was reading to Renzi, Renzi placed his small hand on the page and looked up at Ben. "Can we call Jennifer and tell her you're my daddy now?"

Ben wondered how long he was going to ache for her and be torn apart by just the mention of her name. "I imagine she's out at a party by now, Renzi. I don't think she'll be that interested."

"I think she will," Renzi replied solemnly. "Let's call her."

Ben looked down into irresistible brown eyes and nodded, reaching for the phone and making the call to Weston's, learning from a servant that she had moved back to her apartment. Next he dialed her apartment. He got an answering machine and hung up without leaving a message. "She's not home," he said, wondering if she was dating someone else yet, knowing Weston would do everything possible to see that she did. "Let's get back to the book."

Renzi was studying him intently. He climbed into Ben's lap and wound his small arms around Ben's neck. He smelled like soap and the minty smell of chewing gum as he looked at Ben. "I'm glad you're my daddy."

"I'm glad, too," Ben said, hugging Renzi and closing his eyes as he held the small child against his chest. "I love you, Renzi. You're the most wonderful son in the world."

"I am?"

"You are."

Satisfied, Renzi wriggled and sat down and jabbed the book. "Finish the story."

Ben read, but his thoughts were on Jennifer. Where was she? Was she dating someone else or buried in accounting? He doubted the last.

A banging at the back door set Fella to barking, and Ben
closed the book. "What on earth?" He stood. "I'll be right
back," he said, heading toward the door and glancing at the
clock that showed it to be half-past eight.

Eleven

Ben swung open the door to face Zeb who was covered with mud. "We got trouble, Ben. The earthen dam across Flint Creek is about to go. All the rain has weakened it."

"Dammit. I'll be right there. I'll get Mrs. Morgenson to stay with Renzi," he said, glancing toward the tiny house where his new cook and nanny lived.

"I'll get her. We may be there a long time because rain is predicted late tomorrow."

Ben nodded and closed the door. "Renzi, I've got to go. We have trouble," he called and Renzi ran across the room to follow Ben into his bedroom. While Ben yanked on his boots, Renzi jumped onto Ben's bed and turned somersaults. "Is Mrs. Morgenson coming to stay?"

"Yes, she is."

"Can I sleep in your bed?"

Ben grinned at him. "Sure. I'll tell her you're sleeping in here, but when she says lights out, you have to turn the lights off."

"Aw, Dad, please."

Ben looked at him and wondered how long it would take before he didn't feel a thrill shoot through him when Renzi called him Dad. He crossed the room and leaned over the bed. "C'mere and give me a hug."

Renzi flew into his arms, almost knocking Ben off-balance. "Dad, why don't you ask Jennifer to come up here and why don't you ask her to marry you?"

The question came out of nowhere and caught Ben off guard, momentarily sending a stab of hurt as he glanced at Renzi who flopped back on the bed. "We might ask her here sometime," Ben said, hoping to put Renzi off until he forgot about Jennifer, "but I'm getting used to being a dad right now, okay?"

"Okay. Can I watch television for a while?" Renzi asked, big eyes imploring Ben, and Ben laughed.

"Yep. I think I hear Mrs. Morgenson. Be good and do what she says. And no popcorn in my bed."

"No way, Dad."

Ben laughed and left the room to find the tall, gray-haired woman in his kitchen. Widowed, with grown children who had moved out of state, she had been cooking for a family in Santa Fe when she applied for the housekeeper job and Ben hired her. She seemed good with Renzi and could cook better than anyone on the place.

"Mrs. Morgenson, Renzi can sleep in my bed, and he asked if he could watch television for a while." Ben gave instructions and then got a rain slicker and his hat and left.

He swung into the saddle and headed north, glancing back at the house and looking at moonlight shining on the new foundation that soon would be a room for Renzi. Ben thought about how swiftly his life was changing, but there was one aching void and he wondered if he would ever forget Jennifer. Urging his horse forward, he wanted to catch up with Zeb, his thoughts shifting to the dam. He glanced at the clear night sky and prayed they didn't have rain until they could reinforce the dam.

His gaze swept the land around him and he looked up at the mountain where he and Jennifer had made love; he clamped his jaw closed and shifted his gaze to the darkness ahead.

Dressed in navy slacks and a navy blouse, Jennifer glanced at her watch. Ten minutes after nine—an hour and a half before the plane to Albuquerque. Picking up the carryon, she hurried downstairs.

Before she reached the foot of the stairs, the front door burst open and Weston rushed inside. He stopped as soon as he saw her, closing the door behind him and coming into the hall.

"You can't leave."

She shook her head. "I talked to Dr. Neale. He said you can work if you'll take care of yourself."

"That doesn't have anything to do with your going to New Mexico. Why the hell are you chasing after Ben? He made his feelings clear."

Weston's words stung and she lifted her chin. "If that's the case, I'll come right back here, but I want to talk to him and know how he feels."

"Don't go. If you have to talk to him, we'll get him back."

"No," she said, her pulse beginning to drum because she had never crossed Weston before. His blue eyes sparked with anger and his jaw was thrust out. "Don't send your blood pressure up by arguing," she continued. "And I'm moving back to my apartment. I should have done that long ago."

"Why are you doing this?" he asked suddenly. "All the years you were growing up, the college years and after, we've gotten along perfectly."

"I made few demands and you gave me so much, how could I have been dissatisfied? But it's different now. I love Ben."

"If he loved you, he would have told you. Do you know how many women have been in his life? How casual he is about women? Want me to introduce you to a dozen of them here in this town?"

His words cut because she suspected he was right, but she had to find out for herself.

"Suppose he decides he loves you—after all, he knows you'll inherit a fortune when I'm gone, but until then, he can't give you anything. He's got a ranch that's probably mortgaged to the hilt—and one big disaster and it'll go under. Are you giving up all that you have here for the isolation and hard life of a rancher's wife? *If* he'll marry you?"

"I don't know, Weston," she said, hurting and trying to curb her temper. "I want to find out what his feelings are. Right now, that's more important than my job and what I have here."

"You're young and inexperienced and infatuated with him."

"I don't think what I feel is infatuation. If you'll excuse me, I have a plane to catch."

Weston looked as if he were going to physically prevent her from leaving the house as he stood in her path. He was a large, strong man, and suddenly her heart raced in a panic. This was a side to Weston she had heard about, but had never experienced and it was beginning to frighten her. She tightened her grip on the carryon and the briefcase and started toward the door. When he didn't move, her fear grew as she walked up to him. "Let me go, Weston. You can't hold me here against my will."

He moved closer, his blue eyes filled with rage, his fists knotted on his hips, his navy suit coat pushed open. His face had darkened with anger, and she wondered if he did intend to keep her locked in the house until she missed her plane.

"If I miss this plane, I'll just take another one."

"If you take the flight to New Mexico, you're fired from your job."

She frowned as she stared at him. "Ben told me you could be cruel, but I've never experienced it before."

"I'm trying to keep you from making a colossal mistake and from letting Ben hurt you. And he *will* hurt you. Women mean nothing to him. He's not longing for you or you would have had a phone call."

Doubts rose to assail Jennifer again because for the past week she had debated whether to go to New Mexico or not. "I just have to hear him tell me. You lied to me about your condition. You might be behind Ben's leaving so suddenly and cutting all ties."

"No, I'm not. You'll see I'm right, but you're going to pay a price, Jennifer. I don't have a son any longer. Now I'm losing my daughter. The only child I have is Falcon Enterprises. If you go to Ben, you'll lose your job, you'll lose my benevolence and I'll write you out of the will. You marry him and you won't inherit one dime from me."

"The money isn't that important," she said, tears stinging her eyes because her illusions about Weston and his love were shattering. "I loved you and it wasn't because of your money. If we had been in a small house and you'd had an ordinary job, I would have still loved you as the father that Billy never was."

"Then don't do something stupid now. Don't throw away everything I've given you for a man who cares nothing about you."

Her throat felt tight. "Keep the money, Weston. And the job. I'll never feel the same about it even if Ben sends me home on the next plane."

"What happens if you drive up there to find another woman with him?"

"Then I'll turn around and go."

"You can't come home."

"This isn't home any longer. I wonder if I ever really knew you. You were so good to Mom and to me."

"Your mother was the most beautiful woman I've ever known. I adored her and she was the perfect wife. And I thought I had the perfect daughter until Ben seduced you. You're so like her, Jennifer, in so many ways," he said in a husky voice, and suddenly Jennifer wondered if all his generosity and attention the past few years had been because she reminded him of Callie. He placed his hands on her shoulders. "Don't leave me."

The expression in his blue eyes was as determined as the toughness she had seen in Ben's face at times. As she tried to pull away, Weston's hands tightened. He shook her, and she felt a ripple of shock because he had never physically hurt her.

"You're a little fool, sweet-talked into his bed when you don't have any experience!"

"Let go of me, Weston," she said forcefully and twisted free. With her heart pounding, she brushed past him.

"Don't come back, Jennifer," he said coldly. "Your job just ended and you're not welcome in this house."

She paused with her hand on the doorknob. "Did you tell Ben the same thing?"

"Yes, I did."

"You're going to be very alone, Weston." She stepped outside and closed the door, scared that he would charge out and try to prevent her from leaving. She slid behind the wheel of the car and locked the door, her hand shaking as she turned the ignition. She could still feel where his fingers had bitten into her shoulders.

As she pulled away from the house, she glanced over her shoulder. Sunlight splashed over the white granite and it looked magnificent with pink crepe myrtle and red roses in bloom in flower beds. Tears rolled down her cheeks because she had loved Weston, and until this morning, he had been a good, warm father to her.

Wiping her tears, she glanced at her watch and headed for the airport.

As Jennifer drove away, Jordan Falcon watched her white car turn the corner out of sight. Did she have the briefcase with her? He wished he could have parked close enough to see the front door, but he couldn't risk it.

His pulse raced because he was taking the biggest risk of his life, but he had taken risks before and they had paid, working on Weston's anger at Ben whenever he could. Now Ben was out of the picture forever. If he could get either Weston or Jennifer out, the company would be his!

His heartbeat quickened and he reached for the ignition, starting the motor and swinging into the street, signaling and turning onto the drive, suddenly speeding up until he reached the front door, where he slammed on his brakes and ran up the steps, ringing the bell and pacing back and forth.

Weston opened the door instead of a servant and Jordan burst inside. "Is she still here? Did she take a briefcase with her?"

"Jennifer?" Weston was in his shirtsleeves, his tie pulled loose and his hair in disarray as if he had been raking his fingers through it. He looked angry, and Jordan felt elated.

"Yes, dammit."

"She's gone to the airport. Come into my office where we can talk." Jordan followed Weston, and as soon as they entered the office, Weston closed the door. He looked at Jordan who had stopped in the center of the room and was waiting. "What's the urgency about Jennifer?"

"Has she gone to Ben?"

"Yes. I tried to stop her, but she wouldn't listen."

"No, she wouldn't. We need to get the legal department alerted. She took copies of the Falcon books."

"Why would she do that?" Weston asked, his blue eyes narrowing, and Jordan's pulse raced. He made an effort to keep his voice calm as Weston started across the room toward a chair.

"I've been checking on her since last week when I overheard her talking to Ben. If I'm not mistaken, Ben's on the payroll of his old friend, Garrick Sutherland. I've warned you about the rumors that Sutherland Oil is going to try a takeover of Falcon Enterprises."

Weston whirled around and Jordan braced himself, for a moment his heart pounding wildly in fear because Weston looked as if he would go for his throat. "Damn! She had a briefcase in her hand."

"She's not taking work from the office to New Mexico."

"Damn them both. They'll never get Falcon!"

Jordan started breathing again. *Weston believed him.* "I told you that Ben and Sutherland got together when Ben was here," Jordan reminded him.

Clenching and unclenching his fists, his breathing heavy, Weston nodded. "They'll never get Falcon. You get the legal department working on this. Sutherland isn't much bigger than Falcon."

"Sutherland Oil is bigger, and they can cause us a lot of expense and delays, and she has our books," Jordan said softly. "If you took the company jet, you could get to the ranch before she does on a commercial flight. You could get those books back from Jennifer before she reaches Ben. Of course, she'll deny everything."

"Dammit." Weston swore, his face a dark red and Jordan wondered how much it would take for Weston to have a stroke.

"She and Ben will both deny it if you confront them about it," Jordan said, knowing Weston would accept that as the truth. He would never side with Ben now and hopefully by the time he reached New Mexico, Weston would be in a blind rage. "Want me to call and get the jet ready?"

"Yes," Weston said. As Jordan picked up the phone and punched a number, he watched Weston get a pistol from his desk drawer. With racing pulse Jordan ordered the jet ready and replaced the receiver, looking at the gun in Weston's hand.

"She's going to give me those copies."

"Be careful. Hick sheriffs out in areas like Ben's are going to be on the side of their constituents."

"I'll be careful," Weston said coldly, fury clear in his voice. He leaned closer. "Ben has never done anything except cause me trouble. Never! He's not my son any longer. Get me an alibi, Jordan, in case there's trouble," he said, his blue eyes boring into Jordan, who felt another leap in his heartbeat. "I'll make it up to you."

"Don't worry about a thing," Jordan said. "I'll get back to the office. Call me if you need anything else."

Weston nodded, a muscle working in his jaw, and Jordan turned, leaving the house, his pulse racing. Whatever the outcome, he could always say he jumped to the wrong conclusions and he could claim he had no idea who copied the books. If nothing came from Weston's confronting them, except denials, it would turn Weston against both Jennifer and Ben. And if Weston didn't give them time to convince him of the truth—Falcon Enterprises was the prize!

Twelve

———

Jennifer turned the rental car out of the airport lot and headed north toward I-25. Two hours later, uncertainty gripped her as she wound along the mountain road toward Ben's ranch.

Finally she slowed in front of his log house that looked welcoming, filled with treasured memories of Ben. Her palms were damp with nervousness. Ben was probably working, and the house would be empty. She knocked on the back door, and when no one answered, she opened it, thrusting her head inside.

"Ben?" she called.

"Jennifer? In here," came a muffled call, and she dropped her carryon and the briefcase and rushed toward the living area. The moment she stepped into the room, she halted in shock.

Dressed in dark slacks and a blue shirt, Weston stood in the doorway across from her.

"Where's Ben? How did you get here?" she asked, puzzled and amazed to find him in Ben's house.

"I flew up in our jet then rented a car. I want the copies of my books that you've taken," he said, his voice thick with obvious rage.

"Copies of your books?" she repeated, suddenly confused. "I don't have any—"

"I didn't expect you to confess you did."

"I don't! I brought a carryon and Ben's briefcase—" She stopped, remembering Ben's lunch with Garrick Sutherland. Who knew what Ben would do against Weston. She felt stunned by Weston's charges. When she looked up at Weston, his eyes narrowed and he charged past her.

She followed him. "Weston, I didn't take any records. Jordan gave—" And then she thought about Jordan giving her the briefcase.

Weston had already yanked open the briefcase and pulled up a ledger and flipped it open. She knew what it would contain before he looked at it.

"Weston, you'll have to believe me," she said grimly. "I didn't know—"

"Shut up! You've betrayed me! You—I gave you everything and you betrayed me!" He pulled out a pistol and pointed it at her and Jennifer felt cold, hearing the rage in his voice.

"Get in your car," he said, grinding out the words. Snapping the briefcase closed and carrying it, Weston stepped aside and motioned for her to go through the door.

"Please listen to me," she said as she went outside. Sunshine was warm on her shoulders and breezes tugged at her hair that was fastened with a clip behind her head.

"Slide in the passenger side," he ordered, and when she did, he motioned with the gun. "Now get over. You'll drive."

"I haven't taken any copies of anything. Jordan is deceiving you and trying to stir you up over this," she said, praying it was Jordan and not Ben who had taken the books.

"We're getting away from the house before Ben comes along, and you're going to tell me about Garrick Sutherland. Drive to the highway."

She started the car and turned around to head back the way she had come. "I haven't talked to Garrick Sutherland." She glanced at him, wondering if he could really hurt her, yet since the encounter in the hallway in Dallas she realized he did have a cruel side she had never seen before. And she knew he was obsessed when anything involved his company. When they turned in a bend in the road, she glanced in her rearview mirror, wishing for Ben, but the road was empty behind her.

"Dammit, don't do anything to cause trouble," Weston said, and she looked ahead to see a pickup approaching.

Her window was up and she wished she had it down because if she screamed, she couldn't believe that Weston would shoot her in cold blood in front of anyone. But with the window closed, Weston would never give her a chance to do anything. The pickup was a battered vehicle, badly in need of paint, dented and scratched. It swung around to pull alongside and pass her and her heart missed a beat because it was Todd and he braked to a stop. Renzi was beside him, clambering over Todd and yelling at her.

"Wave at them and roll down your window. Don't do anything you shouldn't, Jennifer," Weston snapped. "They might get hurt."

"Hi, Jennifer! What are you doing here?"

"Tell him not to give away the surprise to Ben that you're here," Weston hissed.

She wondered about bolting from the car, but Weston had become a man she didn't know and she couldn't risk harm to Todd or Renzi.

"Don't tell—" She paused because Renzi scrambled out of the pickup and ran toward her. "Renzi, you go back—"

To her horror, he kept running to her car. "Jennifer! When did you get here?" He slammed his palms against the car door, looking up at her. "You're back!"

"Renzi, get back in the pickup with Todd."

"Just tell the boy to keep your surprise," Weston snapped under his breath.

"Todd, I want to surprise Ben. Don't tell him I'm here. Take Renzi with you."

"Renzi, come on," he called.

"I want to ride with Jennifer."

"Renzi, go with him," she said and saw his mouth turn down.

"Please, Jennifer," he begged, and she felt cold all over as Weston jammed the gun against her side so fiercely that she had to bite back a cry of pain. Weston opened the back door, and Renzi slid into the car. As Todd waved and drove away, she turned to hug Renzi, now terrified about what Weston might do.

"Get going," Weston said.

"Renzi, this is Mr. Falcon, Ben's father."

"How do you do," Renzi said solemnly and Weston ignored him. Renzi opened the window, looking back at Todd.

"Weston, let me take Renzi down to the house and let him out," she begged while she drove.

"No," he said, cold blue eyes meeting hers. She felt as if icy fingers closed around her heart because in that moment she knew he was going to hurt her and Renzi.

"I thought you were a wonderful father," she said as much to herself as to him. "I told Ben you were."

"I can imagine his reply to that. Geoff was my good son and he was killed in an accident. I tried to shower you and Ben with everything, and look what I get for it!" he exclaimed, his voice becoming loud.

"We're not doing anything to harm you." Jennifer wound around a bend and suddenly Weston pointed.

"Take that road."

She glanced at it and remembered the shortcut between Ben's place and the boys' ranch. "That's barely a road, and it may lead to where Ben and the men are."

"Take it," Weston ordered and she turned, smashing bushes and bouncing over a rut, her mind racing for a way to get Renzi out of the car. There could be only one reason for Weston to tell her to take an obscure mountain road.

"Dammit! Stop the car," Weston exclaimed. "The kid threw his shoe out the window. Go get your shoe."

She looked at Renzi who gazed up at her with large eyes, his lips clamped shut.

"Go get your shoe," she said quietly, and he climbed out of the car and trudged back down the lane, hobbling on one shoe, his hands jammed into his pockets.

"Let him go, please, Weston. You can't harm us and expect to get away with it. Please."

"It's too late."

She looked at Weston. "I don't know you at all."

"Shut up, Jennifer." He ground out the words and jammed the gun into her side. She bit back the cry of pain, trying to avoid alarming Renzi any more than he already was. She twisted around to see him stooping over in the road to retrieve his shoe and then he came back and climbed into the car and she drove ahead.

They wound up the mountain, the motor grinding as she shifted into low gear. "This car was never meant for this kind of road," she said, wondering if Weston had become completely unhinged over the imagined threat of losing Falcon Enterprises. Or could there be truth to what he was saying? But it was far easier to suspect Jordan of taking the books. Ben had no interest in the business.

Could she drive into sight of the boys' ranch before Weston did something violent? She gripped the wheel tightly, praying they could drive onto the ranch without his realizing where he was. They were almost at the top of the mountain because ahead she saw the splintered boards of the old mine.

"Pull in there where that building is," Weston ordered. "There may be people there."

He jammed the gun against her again and this time she couldn't keep from crying out. "Weston, please."

"You made your choice this morning. Pull over."

She thought about jamming her foot on the gas, but there was nothing to gain by wrecking the car, and right now, she was Renzi's only hope.

"Stop here," Weston ordered as they slowed on a sunny spot a few yards from a pile of rubble and the ramshackle building. The view was panoramic, but she barely noticed it, glimpsing one of the ranch roads in the distance below.

"Get out and get the kid out."

She paused, turning to look at him. "You'll lose everything if you harm us now. Todd saw you with us—"

"He's the only person who's seen me. I'll have an alibi at home and it'll be his word against mine. Which one of us would be the most suspect?"

"You may have been seen by others," she said, trying to talk to him, hoping that he would calm.

"My witnesses will be credible. I'll be cleared. Do you think I'd really be suspect?"

She knew he wouldn't. Jordan would have an alibi for him. "So now everything will go to Jordan."

"Yes. You and Ben could have had most of it. I worked hard for what I've made and now Ben and you want to take it from me."

"No, we don't." She looked into his eyes and didn't think he would let her leave this place alive. "Don't do this."

"Get out now."

She placed her hand on his wrist, knowing she was taking a chance, but trying to prolong her time with him in hopes something would give her an edge or a way to protect Renzi. "Weston, if I promise to go back with you right now and never talk to Ben, would that change your mind?"

As he studied her, she felt a glimmer of hope. "You know I keep my word," she continued. "I'll work for Falcon, live in Dallas—Ben doesn't know I'm here, so there's no need to tell him anything. And we won't have to worry about Renzi because I can deny anything he says to Ben."

He stared at her as if he were considering what she said and she tried to think of something to do. Weston was too large a man for her to overpower, and in the close confines of the car she might endanger Renzi.

"Please, Weston. I'll go back and it'll be the way it was before."

He shook his head. "I've lost you anyway. Get out or I'll pull the trigger right here in front of him."

Motioning to Renzi, she climbed out. Weston stepped out, the pistol pointed at her. She looked into the muzzle of the gun and knew they had little chance of survival, but she had to try to save Renzi.

Wind whistled through the pines and the air was cool and clear. She heard twigs snap beneath Weston's feet as he came around the car and stopped and then silence came except for the sigh of the wind.

A twig snapped nearby. Frowning, Weston glanced around and Jennifer took the only chance she might have and threw herself at him.

"Run, Renzi! Run!" she screamed. As the child scrambled away she flung herself at Weston's middle. The gun blasted and she felt a burning as she screamed and crashed into Weston. A deep voice yelled just before oblivion.

Ben heard the blast of the gun and everything inside him seemed to clench. He burst through the trees, bellowing in rage as Jennifer crumpled like a rag doll. Renzi ran while Weston faced Ben.

Blind with rage and terror for Jennifer, Ben didn't slow his pace but charged toward Weston, looking down the muzzle of the pistol. "You damned son of a bitch!" Ben said and slammed his fist into Weston, knocking him down. He stomped on Weston's hand and yanked away the gun, glancing at Renzi who stood several feet away watching with wide eyes.

Ben knelt beside Jennifer and turned her over carefully, drawing his breath at the sight of blood darkening her blue blouse. He picked her up carefully. "Renzi," he called and headed back down the mountain, turning his back on Weston, his rage overwhelmed by fear for Jennifer.

"Lady, dammit, how many times do I have to rescue you?" he said. "Hang on, honey. Hang on." Thankful Todd had told him about seeing Jennifer, Ben strode to his Jeep that was parked beneath pines, the door still standing open. He placed Jennifer inside on the narrow back seat. He glanced back once and then picked up Renzi to hug him. "Okay?"

"Yes, Dad," came a small voice as Renzi hugged him in return.

Ben swung him down onto the seat beside Jennifer and ripped off his shirt, wadding it up and placing it against her wound. "Hold this tightly against her shoulder."

As Renzi placed both hands on the shirt, Ben reached for the cellular phone and punched 911. "This is Ben Falcon. I need an ambulance and the police here. My father just shot someone. I'm on my ranch, but I'll head for the highway toward Rimrock. I'm in a Jeep with the lights on. Hurry, dammit."

He turned off the phone and looked at Renzi who sat beside Jennifer. Placing the pistol on the floor, Ben slid behind the wheel and started down the mountain, cursing the rough road with each bounce. He had driven five miles on the highway when he heard sirens.

At the hospital he paced the floor while Renzi sat quietly near a television. A nurse came out of the emergency room to motion to him. "Mr. Falcon, we're taking her to surgery now. The bullet has lodged in a bone high on her shoulder. No vital organs were hit. Someone will tell you when we take her to the recovery room."

He nodded and saw Renzi watching, so he sat down beside the child to explain to him what was happening.

Finally he got the doctor's report that the bullet had been removed. The first few hours after she regained consciousness, she was too groggy and sedated to talk to Ben, but when she dozed and opened her eyes and focused on him, a look of alarm in her features, he guessed she was fully alert.

"Renzi?"

"I'm here, Jennifer," he said, coming closer to the bed and she reached out to squeeze his hand.

"Ben," she said, her voice suddenly sounding shaky again.

"Just a minute, Jenny," he said, taking Renzi's hand and leading him into the hall. Ben knelt to look at Renzi, placing his hands on his shoulders. "You were with her when this happened and I wasn't. Give me just a minute alone with her first and then I'll come get you and you can talk to her. Okay?"

"Yes, Dad," Renzi said, nodding.

Ben's pulse quickened as he returned to her room. Pale, with her hair tangled behind her head, and dressed in a hospital gown, she still looked gorgeous to him.

"Here we are again in a hospital with you coming to my rescue," she said, smiling at him.

All glib answers left him. When he thought about how close he had come to losing her, seeing Weston with the pistol and hearing it fire, watching her slump to the ground, Ben couldn't speak. Tears stung his eyes and his throat was a knot and his hands shook as he sat on the bed and slipped his arms around her waist.

"Don't let me hurt you," he whispered, trying to avoid hugging her hard or touching her shoulder. "God, I'm glad you're safe," he whispered, knowing he needed to wipe his eyes, but unable to take his arms from around her.

She clung to him with her good arm, holding him tightly and he turned his head to kiss her fiercely, his tongue meeting hers, her answering kiss making his pulse jump. She was soft, luscious, and he was already hard for her. Trying to calm himself, he pulled away to look at her.

"How'd you find us?" she asked.

"Why are you here?" Ben asked at the same moment.

"To find out whether you left because you lost interest or because you knew what Weston was giving me."

"I couldn't offer you what he—"

She placed her cool fingers on his mouth, silencing him. "Then we'll never talk about it again." She frowned slightly. "Where is Weston?"

"I slugged him and took the gun. He didn't give me any fight. They called me here at the hospital just a few minutes ago and he's at the sheriff's. They have him in custody."

"Ben, I'm not hurt badly." Her green eyes were wide and clear. "We don't have to press charges."

"He's been cruel, but I didn't know he could lose all control. Was it because you came back to me?"

She shook her head, her gaze going over his face with a deliberation that set his pulse drumming. "No. Jordan told him we were working with Garrick Sutherland for a hostile takeover of Falcon. I didn't know it, but I had a set of Falcon books with me. Jordan told me you'd left something behind."

"Damn Jordan. Maybe he can't lie his way out this time."

"How'd you find us?"

"Todd. I chewed him out for leaving Renzi at the house and he broke down and admitted you wanted to surprise me, but when he told me that you had a man with you and you tried to get Renzi to stay with him, I had a gut feeling that something was wrong. I started back where Todd said he last saw you. I thought I saw a glimpse of a car on the mountain, but I wasn't sure. I was headed for the highway when I passed the shortcut to the Bar-B. I stopped and got out to see if it looked as if someone had driven on it recently. Twigs were smashed, and then I saw a bunch of coins in the road."

"Coins?"

"I asked and Renzi told me about throwing his shoe out the window. He'd seen that done on television. When he picked up his shoe, he dropped the coins. Once I caught another glimpse of the car and this time I had a good view and I thought about the mine. I was coming up on foot when I heard the shot." He stroked her cheek. "I don't want to ever live those moments over again." Feeling joy surge in him, he held her chin. "You are the most gorgeous, sexiest, sweetest female on earth. Just please stop going off mountains and getting shot!"

She smiled at him, the dimple showing and he stood. "Renzi's waiting. I told him just to give me a few minutes alone with you."

An hour later while Renzi stayed at the hospital with Jennifer and nurses fussed over the little boy, Ben entered the adobe building that held the jail and the sheriff's office.

In minutes Ben stood alone in a room that had a table and chairs and bars on the windows. Weston was led in to see him. He had a swollen lip and dried blood on his mouth. He looked pale and dazed and uncertain, something Ben never had seen before. Weston faced Ben.

"You were going to take over my company. You and Garrick Sutherland."

"No, I wasn't. I just saw Garrick for lunch when I was in Dallas. We never talked business."

"He said you'd deny it."

"Jordan," Ben said tiredly. "Jordan always influencing you. You know damned well if I intended to work with Garrick on a takeover, I'd admit it."

A stricken look crossed Weston's face. "Jordan?" He ran his hand through his hair and gazed beyond Ben. "What have I done? I believed Jordan—"

"You've always believed him," Ben said, and Weston met his gaze.

"I almost killed Jennifer—"

"She'll recover. We won't press charges. I don't know about the county attorney. Jennifer will recover and my son is safe. You'll have to live with what you did, Weston."

"Your son? Ben—"

Ben turned around and walked out of the office. He heard Weston call his name again, but he kept going, pushing open the door, wanting to break into a run to get back to Jennifer and Renzi.

Two days later, Ben picked Jennifer up at the hospital. Her hair was caught up with barrettes on either side of her head. She wore a blue cotton blouse and jeans and the bandage on her shoulder showed only a strip of white at the neck of her blouse. As they drove through Rimrock, Ben turned into a hotel and she looked at him with her brows arching in curiosity.

"I want you to myself for a few minutes because when we get to the ranch, there's a welcoming party."

"Oh, Ben, for me?"

He parked and went around to open her door, taking her arm to lead her through the lobby that she barely saw. She was too aware of the tall man at her side. He was dressed in a white shirt, his sleeves turned back slightly, the shirt tucked into his jeans. He looked full of vigor and energy, and in minutes she knew it would all be directed toward her and anticipation made her tingle.

As they rode in the elevator, they weren't alone and they didn't talk. The moment they stepped into the hotel room, he drew her into his arms.

"Lord, it's been an eternity since I had you to myself," he said, taking the barrettes out that held her hair behind her head, and leaning back against the door, spreading his legs to pull her close against him. "I'll try to be careful of your shoulder." His hands shook as he kissed her and peeled away her clothes, and in minutes he stretched on the floor, pulling her down over him, his hands on her hips as he settled her on his throbbing erection.

Jennifer moved on him, her hands on his waist while he stroked her and she cried out in ecstasy. She heard his cry as he thrust deep and hard, holding her hips when he reached his climax. She was in bliss, unaware of discomfort from her shoulder, filled with joy that ran deeper than rapture, a soul-satisfying surety that Ben loved her and had left Dallas without asking her to go with him for her sake. As she straddled him, she gazed down at him. "I love you, Ben."

His hands drifted over her, resting on her hips as he watched her. "I love you, too. Will you marry me?"

"Oh, Ben! Yes! Oh, yes!" Tears of joy stung her eyes as she thought how much she had longed to hear those words.

"Ranch and Renzi and all?"

"Yes!" she said, leaning over him to kiss him, her hands drifting on him until she felt his readiness. "Again? My, you're oversexed!"

"Just crazy over you," he drawled. "I need my pants."

"No, you don't."

"Yes, I do," he said, moving her away and rolling up to yank them to him and fish in the back pocket and produce a small box that he placed in her hand. "I got this in Dallas."

She opened the box and stared at a sparkling diamond ring. Surprised, she looked up at him. "In Dallas?"

He took her hand in his and slipped the ring on her finger while he watched her solemnly, thinking he was the luckiest man on earth. He slid his good arm around her and held her. "I love you," he said in a husky voice.

Jennifer's heart soared with happiness while this time she let the tears fall. "You should have asked me in Dallas. Do you really think an accounting job is more important to me?"

He shook his head. "It wouldn't have been to me, but you were going to inherit half of everything. If you married me, he said he would cut us both out of anything. He said he could give—"

"Never mind. This is what I want," she said, looking into Ben's eyes that were filled again with hunger. "Let's marry soon."

"We can stop at the justice of the peace today."

"No!" she answered, her dimple appearing. "I want Renzi to be a part of it."

"We can get him and stop at the justice of the peace."

"Nope, but we'll marry soon."

"And then when Renzi's settled into a routine and your shoulder is healed," he said, "we're taking a honeymoon." He pulled her down on the floor on her good side. "If you're tired of the floor, there's a bed in this place."

She ran her hand over his hip down along his thigh, across to his erection. "Mmm," she murmured, her fingers circling him. "Ben," she said as he gasped and cupped her breast. "Listen to me."

"Mmm."

"I want Renzi to have a brother or a sister."

Ben paused and looked at her with a twinkle in his dark eyes. "I do too, but *after* our honeymoon. We've had too many damned interferences." He pulled her to him, bending his head to kiss her, promising love.

She wound her good arm around his neck to cling to him, knowing that Ben, her special man, was what was all important in her life.

* * * * *

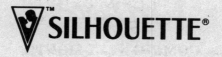

™SILHOUETTE®

Who needs mistletoe when Santa's Little Helpers are around...

SANTA'S LITTLE HELPERS

We know you'll love this year's seasonal collection featuring three brand-new festive romances from some of Silhouette's best loved authors - including Janet Dailey

And look out for the adorable baby on the front cover!

THE HEALING TOUCH	by Janet Dailey
TWELFTH NIGHT	by Jennifer Greene
COMFORT AND JOY	by Patrica Gardner Evans

Available: December 1996   Price £4.99

SILHOUETTE *Desire*

COMING NEXT MONTH

A COWBOY CHRISTMAS   Ann Major

Man of the Month

Born under the same Christmas star, Leander Knight and Heddy Kinney shared the same destiny. Now the handsome cowboy had to stop her Christmas wedding—to *another* man!

MIRACLES AND MISTLETOE   Cait London

Rugged cowboy Jonah Fargo was a scrooge when it came to Christmas—until Harmony Davis sauntered into his life. Could she get him under the mistletoe and make him believe in miracles?

CHRISTMAS WEDDING   Pamela Macaluso

Just Married

Holly Bryant was expected to pose as Jesse Tyler's bride-to-be, not fall for the hard-headed man! But Jesse was a woman's dream come true, even though he swore he'd never settle down…

DADDY'S CHOICE   Doreen Owens Malek

Taylor Kirkland would do anything to win custody of his only daughter. So when captivating Carol Lansing moved into town, Taylor realized there was no better way to get his little girl back than with a beautiful blushing bride by his side…

EVAN   Diana Palmer

Texan Lovers

Ever since she could remember, Anna Cochran had been passionately, shamelessly in love with tall, strapping Evan Tremayne. And although the stubborn man refused to take her seriously, he couldn't deny she awoke a fierce, restless yearning in his hardened heart…

GIFT WRAPPED DAD   Sandra Steffen

Six-year-old Tommy Wilson asked Santa for a dad, so he was thrilled when Will Sutherland showed up in time for Christmas. Now if only Will could convince Tommy's mum he'd make the perfect husband for her!

GET 4 BOOKS
AND A MYSTERY GIFT

Return this coupon and we'll send you 4 Silhouette Desire® novels and a mystery gift absolutely FREE! We'll even pay the postage and packing for you.

We're making you this offer to introduce you to the benefits of Reader Service: FREE home delivery of brand-new Silhouette® romances, at least a month before they are available in the shops, FREE gifts and a monthly Newsletter packed with information.

Accepting these FREE books and gift places you under no obligation to buy, you may cancel at any time, even after receiving just your free shipment. Simply complete the coupon below and send it to:

SILHOUETTE READER SERVICE, FREEPOST, CROYDON, CR9 3WZ.

No stamp needed

Yes, please send me 4 free Silhouette Desire novels and a mystery gift. I understand that unless you hear from me, I will receive 6 superb new titles every month for just £2.30* each postage and packing free. I am under no obligation to purchase any books and I may cancel or suspend my subscription at any time, but the free books and gifts will be mine to keep in any case. (I am over 18 years of age)

D6YE

Ms/Mrs/Miss/Mr _____

Address _____

_____

_____ Postcode _____

mps
MAILING
PREFERENCE
SERVICE

COMING NEXT MONTH FROM
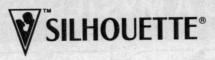 **SILHOUETTE**®

Sensation
A thrilling mix of passion, adventure and drama

LOVER UNDER COVER Justine Davis
CALLAGHAN'S WAY Marie Ferrarella
FIVE KIDS, ONE CHRISTMAS Terese Ramin
A VERY CONVENIENT MARRIAGE Dallas Schulze

Intrigue
Danger, deception and desire

WHITE WEDDING Jean Barrett
HANDSOME AS SIN Kelsey Roberts
HEART VS. HUMBUG M.J. Rodgers
TILL DEATH US DO PART Rebecca York

Special Edition
Satisfying romances packed with emotion

THE BRIDE AND THE BABY Phyllis Halldorson
MR ANGEL Beth Henderson
DADDY CHRISTMAS Cathy Gillen Thacker
A CHRISTMAS BLESSING Sherryl Woods
A GOOD GROOM IS HARD TO FIND Amy Frazier
THE ROAD BACK HOME Sierra Rydell